JUNE WHATLEY

A Window in Time

June Whatley

Copyright © 2022 by June Whatley

Published by Jurnee Books, an imprint of Winged Publications

This book is a work of fiction. Names, characters, places, and incidents are the product of the author's imagination and are used fictitiously. Any resemblance to actual events, locales, or persons, living or dead, is coincidental.

All rights reserved including the right to reproduce this book or portions thereof in any form whatsoever – except short passages for reviews – without express permission.

ISBN: 979-8-8690-6377-9

Acknowledgements

Many thanks to my wonderful Beta Readers, Kay Wojack and Beverly Basham Smith, your input, as always, is invaluable. You push me to make me better. Thank you! Blessings!

And my never ending thanks to my Lord and Savior Jesus Christ, to Father God and to his Holy Spirit. I know that you have answered my prayers to make my stories better and more exciting, and I hear you many times adding details to my books. Thank you so much! I love you and pray that my books draw people to you and change lives for your glory.

Fifteen Years Earlier:

As Mican (then age fourteen) rose to his feet a mist began to form behind Abba's throne. It became like a screen in a movie theater. Mican stood speechless. Before his eyes, a picture of himself as a baby appeared. Next, he watched the pictures, as he grew into a toddler and then as a young child.

The pictures advanced all the way to his current age of fourteen, but didn't stop there. His image continued to change and mature until he saw himself as a man, dressed in a suit, and talking to some people in what appeared to be a large meeting room in an office building.

"This is how I see you even now, my son. I know you as you were, as you are, and as you shall be. The man you are becoming pleases me very much."

As the mist faded, Mican said, "Thank you Abba, but why did you show me this?"

"I want you to know that you have a bright future, just as your Grammy told you. Stay close to me, as I know you will. It will ensure your future will be a bright one."

Mican smiled. "Thank you, Abba."

"My pleasure, son. You may be seated."

He took his seat once again, as Abba called his brother's name. "Ashton, will you stand before me."

Ashton (then age thirteen) promptly stood. Again, behind the throne a mist appeared. He held his breath. The face of a baby appeared, next the image changed to a small child, then all the way to his present thirteen-year-old self.

Again, the pictures continued to age and mature, like Mican, Ashton watched himself as he became an adult. He couldn't help but comment. "In this picture, it looks like I am surrounded by family, friends, and children. The scene looks like it's at Christmas and I'm in a lovely home."

Abba smiled. "That is true, my boy."

In the picture he stood in front of a large window, though it was snowing outside, the room inside appeared warm and cheerful. The people around him seemed loving and joyful. A calm feeling came over him. "Wow, I feel amazing, even now, just seeing this."

"Ashton, my warrior, you have grown so much. I am very pleased. You, more than your brother and sister, have worried about being loved and accepted. Know this, my son. You are deeply loved. You have a bright and wonderful future ahead of you, if you stay close to me, as I know you will."

Tears filled the rims of his eyes. "Thank you, Abba. You're my best friend."

As he took his seat, Shayla (then age eleven) popped up before the King could call her name.

He tossed his head back and laughed. "Excited, are we?"

"Yes Sir, I want to see." The mist began to form behind the throne. Shayla's pictures moved across the screen. First as a baby, then the images changed, and changed again. They zipped right past her eleven-year-old-self until she saw her image as a mature, lovely, young woman. In the picture, she appeared to be in her early thirties. Behind her stood a man holding a small child, but they were blurred by the mist. Shayla squinted and complained. "Abba, I can't see what they look like."

"I know, little one, but that is all I want you to know at this time. If you knew more, you would constantly be trying to make it come to pass. Still I want you to know you have a nice future and a family to come. Keep your eyes on me. Wait for *me* to work it out. It will be *awhile*, but wait, Shayla. Remember, don't run ahead of my Spirit."

"But how will I know?"

The King leaned forward on his throne. "The same way you knew to call on me and how to apply my word to your life. Trust my Spirit to guide you."

Shayla smiled. "Thank you, Abba." She returned to her seat.[i]

Chapter 1

Present Day

A soft tapping at the door drew Shayla's attention, she glanced up from her paperwork. "Benji Perez![ii] What a pleasant surprise. What are you doing here in Sallis?"

A handsome young man with a gleaming smile, strode cockily through the doorway. "Look at you, Officer McKnight! You look so sharp in your copper uniform."

A scrapping noise accompanied her chair being propelled away from the desk. "Give me a hug, you rascal and tell me why you're here."

He knit his brows together. "I hope this isn't inconvenient."

She walked around her desk, stretched out her arms and draped them around his shoulders. "Not at all. I'm glad to see you, tell me the meaning of this gigantic surprise."

"Shay, do you have time for lunch? I want to talk to you about something."

Leaning back to see Benjamin's face, she turned her head slightly to the side. "That sounds ominous."

His hands lifted, palm up. "Not really Shay, it's nothing bad, just another surprise, you might say."

She clapped him on the shoulder and nodded. "Okay, but let me clock out first, give me thirty seconds."

True to her word, half a minute later, she returned with her cap tucked under her arm. "Where do you want to go?"

They walked through the main room, flanked by desks on each side, men looked up and stared at the two as they made their way to the entrance.

Benji pushed the exterior door open and held it for Shayla. "How about that Mexican restaurant right over there," he pointed, "on Walnut Street."

She perched her cap on her head. "Sounds great to me, but I'll have to take the squad car and meet you there."

His hands flew up at his sides. "You've got to be joking," he pointed again, "I can see the restaurant from here."

Laughter betrayed her joke. "You can't expect me to walk a whole block and a half back to the office after I've filled up on fajitas, can you?" She clapped her hand on his back. "I'm only joking, we can walk, but start talking, buster."

A slight lull in the conversation drew Shayla's eyes toward her young friend. "What's up, Benji, you know you can tell me anything."

His shoulders tucked up toward his ears and he ducked his head. "I know Shay, but I don't know where to start."

Poking him with her elbow, she grinned. "Start at the beginning, silly goose, but tell me."

"Okay, you remember when I was five?" A burst of laughter disrupted the serious countenance on Benji's face.

Shayla's wide smile warmed his heart. "Oh, my goodness, does this go that far back?"

Benjamin stopped and turned to face her. "Do you remember when I was five and I tried to write a love note to you on your mom's car window with soap?"[iii]

She stopped and faced him with eyebrows knit tight. "I remember," she giggled, "but I'm pretty sure my mom has forgiven you by now."

He plopped his hands at his waist. "You're not making this easy for me, Shay."

She pressed her lips together, tucked her hands behind her back, pulled her face to a serious pose and stared down at the sidewalk. "Sorry, Benji, go ahead."

"Okay, when my mom had cancer, one day I was sitting on the curb in front of my house. You came by and without even asking, you knew something was wrong and you sat down beside me and talked."

She glanced to the side and nodded. "I remember."

"From that moment on, I knew that I loved you

and I told you that I wanted to marry you."

Her mouth flew open as she faced him. "Benji, this isn't a marriage proposal, is it?"

"Now, don't freak out on me, Shay, I'm only twenty-one. This is me trying to tell you that a while back, I met someone that you know, her name's Holly."

"Holly, hmmm."

"You knew her as Hobbles."[iv]

She spun in front of him with a huge smile, pulled her hands from behind her and grabbed his shoulders. "Oh, my gracious, how is she? And how did you meet?" She still faced him and continued walking backwards.

"She's doing great. You remember the police officer who drove you go get Holly?

"Yes, Andy Davis."

Benji stopped. "Right, well Officer Davis was promoted and married the lady dispatcher you met named Samantha."[v]

Shayla stopped, pulled her hands up in front of her chest and squeezed them together tight. "Oh, that's wonderful."

Benjamin started to walk again. "Well, Andy Davis and Samantha adopted Holly."

Shayla walked along beside him. "That's more wonderful news," she clapped, "so, when do we get to the ominous part?"

"Not yet, there's more. An orthopedic surgeon, from church, did surgery on Holly's injured foot and fixed it for free. She can walk perfectly normal now."

"That's even more great news." She glanced at him. "Go on."

"Then Andy was offered the position of Chief of Police in Arlo, where I live, so he, Samantha, and Holly moved there about three years ago. I happened to bump into them at church the day Holly gave her testimony."

Shayla's eyes welled up with tears, she held her hands up and placed them over her nose and mouth. Her muffled voice said, "So, she's a Christian now!" She paused, her hands came to her sides and she looked at the sidewalk, then glanced at Benji, her voice crackled, "that's wonderful. It's so fulfilling to hear that God is redeeming the lives of those abused children."

Benji placed his hand on her shoulder. "Yes, it is, and in her testimony, she mentioned a girl named Shay who helped to rescue her and a bunch of others who were being trafficked."

Shayla quietly nodded, tears filling the rims of her eyes. "I'm overwhelmed at the thought that Abba used me in that way."

"When she mentioned your name," Benji stared into her eyes, "I was so excited to meet them that they invited me over for lunch. That's when … " He paused.

Shayla tipped her head. "When what, Benji?"

Benjamin's chin dropped to his chest. "That's when I started having feelings for Holly. She's such a strong beautiful Christian, she's just like you Shay, she was like a magnet to me."

Shayla placed her hand on his arm. "Oh, Benjamin, that's great news too, she's just about your age, isn't she?"

He lifted his face to meet her gaze. "Yes, but I

always said I was going to marry you," and his chin fell again.

She smiled gently. "You silly, gopher, get out of that hole you're in. You were a five-year-old kid back then, I never considered it an engagement."

He spread his arms out to the side. "But I really thought I was going to marry you, Shay."

She tipped her head back and laughed, but gave him a side hug. "Don't you have to have my permission first?" and giggled. "I think it's wonderful that Holly's a Christian, that she has a home with a good family and now she's found a great guy to love her. Benji, I couldn't be happier for Holly, or for you."

"Really, Shayla?"

"Absolutely! And by the way," she grinned, "have you written her a soap love-note yet?"[vi]

"That's not funny, Shayla!"

She giggled. "I think it kinda is, Benji." She laughed again and slapped him on the back. "I love you like a brother, Benjamin Perez. Now let's go pig out, no cop pun intended, on some fajitas."

Chapter 2

More Surprises to Come

After lunch, Benjamin escorted Shayla back to the Police Station. Out front, she leaned in to give him a big hug.

At that moment, an old truck rumbled up next to the sidewalk. "Hey lady copper, what does that kid have that I don't?"

Without any hesitation, she flung her stinging reply at him. "Manners! A brain! Get lost, Devin before I arrest you for being annoying!"

His truck pulled away as laughter rolled out of his window.

Benji chuckled and headed to his car. "Bye, Shay! I love you!"

"I love you too, Benji."

The large windows on the front of the red brick building gave her fellow officers a full view of the sidewalk and parking lot.

When she pulled the door open, removed her cap and stepped inside, several *Ooooo's* came from all directions.

"Knock it off you, countrified bumpkins. That boy's like one of my brothers. Not another word out of any of you, or I'll call your mommas, the whole lot of you."

One officer chuckled. "I saw Devin out there too, is he getting jealous? He follows you all over town, you know."

She wheeled around to face him. "Charlie, I know your momma from church, do you want me to call Martha?"

He looked at his desk. "No, ma'am, Shayla."

As she walked on through, Officer Stanley Marcum whispered. "We must've hit a nerve."

She turned and glared at him. "You did, you low class toad and I won't stand for it. Do you hear me?"

The Chief walked in. "You won't stand for what,

Officer McKnight?"

The others stood to attention and she spun to face him and barked out her reply. "Only a little correction of a disrespectful remark, sir."

"Good for you, McKnight. It's time these boys learned a little respect."

Shayla stood erect, but smiled. "Thank you, sir."

"Now, Officer McKnight, I was going to ask you into my office, but since these boys need a reminder of what a good Copper is, I'll talk to you right here." He lifted a piece of mail to Shayla's eyelevel. "I've received a request that you be released from your responsibilities here in Sallis …"

Her mouth flew open and her hands flew out from her sides. "But sir, what have I done wrong?"

The Chief grinned. "As I was trying to say, McKnight, I've been requested to release you, so you can join the next class of students at Quantico? Seems you've impressed some people who are mighty high-up, young lady."

Jaws dropped around the room, including Shayla's. "I've—you've—I'm …"

"Sit down before you fall down, McKnight." He chuckled and pushed the piece of paper her direction. "Here's the letter for your perusal, but I think you would be nuts to turn this down. There's a number you can call. You can use my office for privacy when you gather your wits."

She took the paper and dropped into a chair. Every eye in the room was on her. She lifted the letter and read to herself.

Dear Chief Hansen:

We have been notified that an officer in your department has shown exemplary skill and discipline. She (Officer Shayla McKnight) has been requested by an, as-yet-unnamed department, to attend the upcoming class of trainees at Quantico.

We strongly suggest that, following an immediate promotion, you allow this officer to leave your department to further her career at a higher level of service.

To obtain further information, Officer McKnight

has three days to contact us for details regarding this assignment. The number is in the letterhead.

Your leadership has had much to do with this officer's success. You are to be commended.

Sincerely,
Director ONE (Onboard New employees)
Quantico, VA.

The letter and Shayla's hands collapsed into her lap, her mouth still open.

Chief Hansen stared at her. "Officer McKnight, you will be sorely missed in this department. I suggest you go home and talk with your family. This is a big decision, but an opportunity I believe you must accept. You have the rest of the afternoon off and tomorrow too with pay, you'll need to pack." He smiled. "Come in on Wednesday morning at nine for a short promotion ceremony before you leave us and of course, your family is welcomed to attend."

Around the office, whispers echoed. "Promotion!" then silence.

The momentary quiet was split by one pair of hands clapping. The dispatcher stood behind the large front desk, slowly popping her hands together.

The Chief joined in and one-by-one the officers stood and joined the applause.

Shayla's eyes were wide and her mouth remained slightly open. When the clapping died down, Shayla rose. "Thank you," and staggered toward the Chief's office and followed him in. "Sir, I don't know what to say."

Hansen smiled. "Say, thank you, McKnight. Now you can use my phone to call the number on the letter, then go home. That's an order."

"Yes, sir!"

At home, her mother's surprised voice greeted her. "Hey, honey, you're home two hours early, is everything alright?"

No answer came, so Mom turned and peered into the foyer.

Shayla stood there blank-faced, with her cap under her arm and a letter in her hand.

Candice got up from the sofa and dashed toward her. "Honey, what's wrong?"

Her stepfather heard the concern in Candice's voice and jumped from his chair.

Shayla lifted her hand and Tom Phillips reached for the letter. It took mere seconds to read and he smiled and shoved it at his wife.

Mom read the letter and her mouth flew open. "What? What on earth? That's great! — This is horrible! You'll have to move to Virginia. My baby! My last little chick-a-dee is flying the coop."

Tom placed his arm around his wife. "Honey, you knew this would happen sooner or later. Shayla's twenty-six, she can't stay here forever. We were blessed that she chose a local college and could live at home and then she joined the local Police Force, but we knew it wouldn't be forever."

Candice's face held the same dazed look as her daughter's.

Shayla turned to her stepdad. "But dad, do you think I should go?"

He stepped toward her and placed his hand on her

shoulder. "Well, honey, like every other decision, it's up to you, but I think you'd be daft if you passed this up."

Her eyes glared at him. "But I don't even know who, or why, or how this is happening."

He glanced at the letter again. "Haven't you called the number they gave you?"

"I called, but all they could tell me was that I've been recommended for Quantico. Their classes start a week from today, and after my basic courses, I'll have two tracts to choose from."

His eyebrows scrunched. "What tracts?"

"The Principal Research and Training Facility for the FBI, or the FBI's Hostage Rescue Team."

"Okay, that's a start, we know the sponsoring agency is the FBI, let me call Max and see what the two of us can find out."

Tom pulled out his cellphone and hit speed dial. "Max, we have a situation, can you come over?" He smiled. "No, no one's life's in danger."

Moments later, the rumble of a jeep belonging to

Tom's oldest and dearest friend, greeted their ears, he leapt from the vehicle, bounded up the steps and dashed to the open door where Tom and Candice stood smiling. "What the bog-flap's going on over here, Philly? What's the problem?"

Candice stepped aside. "Come in, Max."

Shayla still stood in the same spot with her mouth ajar and her eyes glazed over.

Max pointed. "What's wrong with the Kitten Copper?"

Tom laughed and lifted the letter for him to read. "Seems the lady's been tapped for Quantico."

Max smiled and took the paper. "Say what!"

Chapter 3

Additional Info

It took an hour and multiple phone calls, but between Max and Tom's contacts, they ascertained that someone, somewhere, had put a flea in the ear of the head of a new FBI program. This division would liaise with the U.S. Marshals Service on a series of various initiatives, including sting operations to bust existing trafficking rings. Acting on this information, the new department head specifically requested Shayla to train at Quantico and be prepared to join his new team.

Shayla stared at her stepdad and Max. "But why me?"

Seated on the sofa with her daughter, mom took Shayla's arm and turned toward her. "Probably because of all those kids you rescued when you were only seventeen, sweetie."

Shayla shook her head. "But God did all of that and that was almost ten years ago."

With his foot propped on the hearth of the gray stone fireplace, her stepdad grinned. "Well, you didn't expect to be tapped for Quantico at age seventeen, did you?"

He and Max laughed.

She pulled herself up from the sofa and plopped her hands on her hips. "I didn't expect to be *tapped* as you put it, for Quantico, ever. I just wanted to be a good police officer here in Sallis."

Tom walked to the couch and took her by the hand. "And you've done that, honey, now your training, experience and character have been recognized and it's time to go into the world and let your light shine."

Her face heated up. "But I'm not ready!"

Max folded his enormous arms and laughed. "You will be after you've finished Quantico, I guarantee it."

"But … But I have to be there in a few days."

Mom stood, placed her hand on her daughter's shoulder and smiled. "Then you need to start packing. I've called the family and invited them over for dinner tonight, so you can share the good news; and Tom, will you get Shay's suitcase out of the attic, please?"

Shayla stared at her. "Mom, they'll probably provide everything I need, once I get there."

Max and Tom looked at each other and burst out laughing again.

Chapter 4

Family Dinner

In the dining room, with its large picture window that looked out onto the beautiful, wooded creek, the family seated themselves around the heavy, rustic table, joined hands and bowed their heads for prayer.

Thomas Phillips began, "Dear Heavenly Father, thank you for this wonderful family you've given me, for my beautiful wife, our great children and my dear friend Max. Bless this food and thank you for Shayla's good news, in Jesus' name, amen." When he opened his eyes, every face at the table was turned toward him. He chuckled.

Mican and the others immediately faced Shayla. "Shay, what news, what's going on?"

She dropped her hands into her lap and stared at her plate. "Well, I've been released from the police force and."

Four gasps went up.

Ashton leaned in. "You've been what? And why?"

She glanced at her brother and laughed. "I did the same thing, I interrupted Chief Hansen when he tried to tell me the news."

Mican's wife Madelaine[vii] scooted to the edge of her seat. "What news, Shay?"

Shayla looked at her. "My Chief received a letter requesting that I be released from duty," she scanned the other faces, "so I could go to Quantico for training."

Ashton plopped his folded arms onto the table. "Why didn't you tell us you'd applied? That's awesome, sis. Some people say that only about twenty percent of applicants get accepted, some estimates say only about six percent get in, it's very competitive."

Her hands rose and her palms flipped up. "But I

didn't apply."

Mican leaned toward her and chimed in. "I don't understand. You didn't apply? Well, then," he held his hands palm up too, "how …?"

His sister grinned. "I know, crazy, right?" and she laughed.

Tom filled in the gap. "It seems that our girl has a benefactor that's given her name to the head of a newly forming FBI Task Force. Your mom and I think it's related to Shayla being involved in rescuing all those kids several years ago."

Ashton tipped his head up and pointed to the ceiling. "I thought that was, you know, Abba who did that." Then he flashed a smile at his stepdad, "did Abba speak to the guy at the FBI?"

Tom Phillips nodded and laughed. "Now that *would* be a good thing, but all we know for sure is that the head of Cease and Desist, that's the proposed name of the new program, said someone high up has been keeping an eye on Shayla's career and put in a good word for her."

Mican sat up straight. "That could be Abba," he

laughed and pointed to the ceiling again, "he's high up."

Chuckles erupted around the table.

Mr. Phillips continued. "That's true, but I think he meant someone in one of the agencies in a high-up position, he mentioned a Rear Admiral in the Coast Guard, a local Tennessee Police Chief, another Police Chief in Idaho and someone in the U.S. Marshals Service."

Shayla's glazed eyes turned toward her stepdad. "That would be Beau."

With one elbow on the table, Max placed his other hand on the corner and leaned back. "Hmmm, Beau is it?"

Flashing him a scrunched mouth and tight knit eyebrows, Shayla insisted. "Stop it Uncle Max. He was a nice man who helped rescue me and some other kids, he was undercover so he said to call him Beau, all right?"

He winked at Philly and risked another comment. "Me thinks she doth protest too much," and burst out laughing.

The clearing of a throat at the end of the table caught his attention. "Max, I think we've teased Shayla enough, we need to eat before the food gets stone cold."

Max's face flashed red. "Yes, ma'am, Candice. Sorry, Shayla."

Mican nodded too and grinned. "Yes, ma'am and please pass the potatoes."

Tom started the line, piling his plate with roast and passing it on. Before long a full complement of roast beef, mashed potatoes, gravy, green beans and salad had passed through everyone's hands.

After dinner, Shayla leaned back in her seat and moaned. "Oh, my goodness, mom, that was so good."

Candice reached and patted her daughter's arm. "It's the least I could do for you and the family before you leave, I'm already feeling sad."

Ashton leaned forward so he could see around his wife Bailey.[viii] "Shay, when do you leave?" He turned his smile to his wife, "and Bay, if I can take a couple of days off from work, would you mind if I drove to Quantico with her?"

Bailey nodded toward Shayla. "That'll be fine, but only for Shay-girl. She's the best."

Mican turned to his wife. "Would you mind if I went with them, Maddy? It'll be our last chance to visit together before Christmas."

Madelaine nodded. "Sure, sweetie. I'd be happy to know that you're with Shay and Ash, I'm sure I can stay with granddad while you're gone." She winked at Max. "Right, Grandpa?" She turned back to Mican. "Just don't stay gone too long." She kissed his cheek. "I'll miss you way too much."

Shayla shrugged and lifted her hands. "Don't I have a say in this?" Then she grinned, "I'd love to have my bubbas ride with me, but how will you get back home?"

Mican gave her a playful tap on the shoulder. "You don't worry your pretty little head about that, Sissy." He laughed and looked at Madelaine, until Shayla gave him a punch of knuckles on the top of his arm. The corners of his mouth dropped, as he whipped back toward her and rubbed his arm. "Ow! What was that for?"

"For being a chauvinist, you know very well that I can take care of myself and don't ever call me Sissy again."

"Sorry, sis, I was only kidding."

"Okay, you two, knock it off." Mom scanned the faces around the table, "one more thing, everybody, Shayla will receive," she grinned, "a promotion to sergeant, in a brief ceremony, Wednesday morning at nine, before she officially leaves the Police Department. Can any of you come?"

Glances side-to-side and nods confirmed that most were sure they could be there.

Mom laced her fingers together with her forearms on the edge of the table and grinned. "Good, we'll all go out for lunch afterwards." She pushed her chair back. "Now that we have that settled, who's going to help with the dishes?"

Her husband stood and lifted his plate. "I think we should let the young people off-the-hook tonight," he flashed a grin at his friend, "don't you agree, Max?"

With a full belly and his arms resting on his abdomen, Max looked up. "Sure thing, Tommy-Boy, let's assist your filly with the dish removal process."

Shayla cocked her head, looked at Max and laughed. "Uncle Max, I haven't heard you call dad Tommy-Boy in a long time, what gives?"

"I don't know, darlin,' feeling a little nostalgic, I guess." He stood and stared at her, "and envious, if I'm honest. You're starting a new adventure and mine is coming to an end. All I have waiting for me in my future are great grandkids from Mican and Maddy," He winked at Madelaine, "not that I'm rushing them."

At that moment, Maddy giggled. "Well, I don't want to rain on Shayla's parade or anything."

Candice dropped a dish in the sink and wheeled around. "What? What are you saying? Are you?"

Madelaine hooked her arm in Mican's and nodded. "Yes, Mom, you and Philly are going to be grandparents and Max will be a great-grandpa." Maddy looked at all the open mouths around the room. "And there's Uncle Ashton, Aunt Bailey and Aunt Shayla. Surprise!" She directed her eyes to Shay. "I hope you don't feel like I'm stealing your thunder, but granddad was busting at the seams to tell everyone and I wanted to tell the family before you left. I thought this might be better than after your ceremony Wednesday."

"Oh, my goodness, Maddy. That's great news and you're not raining on my parade, you're simply watering the flowers in my garden." She leapt to her feet and dove across her brother. "Give me a hug." She wrapped her arms around Madelaine and both girls giggled.

With arms extended wide, Candice bolted toward them. "My turn."

Following the hugs, Maddy added, "I'm a little more than five months along, I was afraid everyone would notice how round I'm getting, so I've been wearing baggie clothes. Since we lost a baby last year, I didn't want anyone to get their hopes up until we were sure."

Chapter 5

The Copper Scroll

Standing in the foyer, before the others left for their respective homes, Mican made another announcement. "With Shayla's news and our news about the baby, I guess now is as good a time as any to tell everyone that I've received an offer to go to the Middle East to work on a new project called the Copper Scroll." He chuckled and pointed at his sister, "not a copper like you, Shay, but a real scroll made out of copper that archeologists found."

Chuckles echoed in the vaulted ceiling.

"Archeologists were exploring the Qumran caves, where the Dead Sea Scrolls were found. It's a site in the West Bank that's managed by Israel's Qumran National Park,[ix] anyway, they stumbled upon a hidden chamber they labeled, Cave Three."[x]

"Oooo, that sounds exciting," Bailey laughed and lowered her voice, "a hidden chamber."

"It really is, Bailey, but for more reasons than just that one. This scroll was found in a sealed chamber in the back of a cave they had already explored. Someone accidentally knocked a hole in the thin wall and saw that there was a recess behind it. They excavated the wall and on a shelf to the left of the opening, they found a scroll, it took time to open because the copper was frail and brittle, the scroll was also coded and had to be decoded, once they had the breakthrough, they discovered that it's a list of silver and gold items that were buried, to protect them from being looted before the temple was plundered in 70 A.D. The Copper Scroll is currently housed in the Jordan Museum in Amman[xi] and I've been invited to take part in the research."

His family clapped and Bailey whooped.

Ashton ran his hand through his hair. "Why is it housed in Jordan if it was found in the park owned by Israel?"

"A long-standing agreement has caused a slight problem, Israel holds some of the Dead Sea Scrolls, but Palestine claims ownership. All I know is the museum is going to allow me to be involved in the research of the Copper Scroll."

Mom reached for a hug. "That's fantastic news, Mican. When do you think you'll leave?"

"It's probably about six months away, after the first of the year, I have to raise the funds for the trip and my expenses while I'm there. You know university budgets, research out of the country is on your own dime, or you raise the money before you go, I just wanted to let you all know that it looks like it's going to happen and I'm really excited."

Chapter 6

Promotion

Wednesday morning, barricades stood at the intersection of Church and Walnut Streets, with orange barrels at the other end of Walnut, blocking traffic both directions. A large crowd of people gathered in front of the Police Department for Shayla's promotion ceremony. Under a very warm July morning sky, chairs had been set-up with the station as the backdrop. Following the presentation of flags, the national anthem and an opening prayer by the Chaplin, Chief Hansen called Shayla forward. "Officer Shayla McKnight, please join me."

Looking crisp and professional in her dress blue uniform, with her hair in a tight knot at the base of her neck, Shayla stepped onto the sidewalk next to the Chief.

"Officer McKnight, in recognition of your exemplary service to the city of Sallis, Tennessee, and being requested by people so high up, that I value my career too much to refuse them," people snickered, the Chief smiled and continued, "I have the honor of promoting you to the rank of Sergeant and the sad displeasure of releasing you from our service to attend classes at Quantico." He faced Shayla and handed her a new set of bars. "Sergeant McKnight, your integrity, professionalism and your winning personality will be sorely missed at the Sallis Police Department. You have been a credit to the town, to our department and to your family. Go in good health and with our blessings." He reached for her hand.

When Shayla grabbed his hand in return, the onlooks, including her fellow officers stood and cheered.

Chief Hansen saluted Shayla and bellowed, "Dissss-missed."

A throng of people headed for her, but before she

was surrounded, she noticed a man across the street from the Mexican restaurant standing in the shade, watching. She couldn't make out his features, but he seemed vaguely familiar, then the crowd of well-wishers reached her, in the mob was Charlie and his mom.

Martha leaned in for a hug. "Congratulations, sweetie, and Charlie told me you threatened to call me." Martha giggled. "Thanks for helping me keep him straight, you'll be missed, my dear."

Shayla gave her a kiss on the cheek. "Thank you, Martha, I'll miss everyone here," she whispered in her ear, "even Charlie, but don't tell him I said so," she leaned away and smiled. "But I'll be back. My family's here, my friends are here and my roots are here. You'll see me again."

Martha smiled. "For a while I had hoped you might be my daughter-in-law someday."

Shayla drew her head back and frowned dramatically. "Me and Charlie? No way, I know he's a good guy, but I'd have to continually box his ears."

Martha laughed. "It would be welcomed, dear.

I'm getting too old to keep it up."

Shayla's head tipped back as she laughed.

At that moment she noticed the Chief behind Martha. Shayla snapped to attention.

"At ease, Sergeant McKnight," he smiled, "I meant every word of what I said, including the fact that if I didn't value my career so much, I would've refused to let you go, but you are meant for greater things than staying here in our tiny town. Be blessed, young woman!"

She extended her hand. "Thank you, sir, serving under your leadership has been a privilege."

Others crowded in, so the Chief nodded, smiled and backed away.

After an hour of hugs and handshakes, Max and Tom Phillips, each seized an elbow.

Max yelled, "Sorry folks, the Sergeant needs some donuts."

The crowd cackled, but gave way.

Her stepdad leaned to her ear. "Your mom's made reservations at the Cookie Jar Cafe,[xii] are you ready for your final meal in town before you leave tomorrow?"

The corners of her mouth sagged. "Oh dad, stop it, that sounds so final!"

Max laughed. "Yeah, Philly, she'll only be gone twenty weeks, don't freak the Kitten Copper out."

She turned to him and one eyebrow rose. "That's Sergeant Kitten Copper to you, mister."

He and Tom howled with laughter.

Chapter 7

Lunch

The Cookie Jar Café welcomed them and they were seated at the long table in the center of the room to the right of the door. As Mom had requested, glasses of ice were placed at each seat and two pitchers of the Cookie Jar's amazing sweet tea were positioned, one at each end of the long table, along with two baskets of their fresh, homemade rolls.

Bailey distributed the small bread plates and reached for a roll and butter. "I'm starving!"

Mom laughed. "You're eating for two now, Bailey."

Max patted his belly. "Me too, I'm eating for me

and this bulge that hangs over my belt these days." He retrieved a roll from the basket closest to him. "It's been hours since breakfast."

Mican flanked Shayla on her right. He placed his arm on the back of her chair and looked at her. "Max and dad will pack your car this evening. All you'll need to do is pack clothes for warm, mild and very cold weather. It can get pretty nippy in Virginia in December, you'll probably need your boots and heavy coat, before graduation that is."

Shayla's hands flipped palm up. "But won't they issue everything I need when I get to Quantico?"

Ashton chirped in from her left. "FBI school's not like the military exactly. You'll get your basic uniforms, your exercise clothes, plus a really cool jogging suit, but you'll have plenty of time to wear your civvies. Just be prepared, that's all Mican's saying."

Her eyebrows tugged down in the middle. "What are Civvies?"

"You know, sis, civilian clothes, civvies."

Her eyes darted side-to-side and she lifted her palms. "How do you two know so much about Quantico?"

Both brothers chuckled.

Ashton lifted his palms to imitate his sister. "The Internet, of course."

Madelaine and Bailey sat across from their husbands and laughed.

Shayla glanced their direction and just behind Bailey, she noticed through the window, a man in a cowboy hat who seemed to be looking at them, but as soon as she noticed him, he turned and headed toward the steps.

"Ashton, did you see that man on the porch?"

He looked around. "What man, Shay?"

"The one in the cowboy hat, I think I saw him after the ceremony this morning."

At that moment, Bailey leaned on the table, she faced Madelaine and grinned, then faced Shayla. "Maddy and I gladly release our dreamboats to escort their beloved sister," she lowered her chin, "and my best friend, I might add, to the next level of her adventure."

Candice applauded. "Well said, Bailey."

Max lifted his water glass. "Here, here! We love you, Sergeant Kitten Copper."

Mican jumped back in the conversation. "So, in the morning, Ash and I will meet you at Mom's a little before five for breakfast," he glanced at their mother, "if that's okay?"

She nodded. "Of course, and Madelaine and Bailey are welcome too."

Max turned her direction and presented a cheesy grin.

Candice laughed. "Of course, you're welcome, Max, the whole family can come see Shayla and the boys off."

Ashton picked up where his brother left off. "We'll take turns driving and that should make it an easier trip."

Shayla's eyebrows squeezed down. "But how will you guys get back? The bus is too slow and airfare is too expensive."

Mican laughed and held up his thumb. "Don't

worry about us, I'm sure these will work."

Very dramatically, her words scolded him. "You—will not—do that!"

Laughter burst out around the table.

Mom reached around Ashton and patted her on the shoulder. "Don't worry sweetheart, your dad and I have a plan."

"But mom!"

"Shush now, it's all under control, honey." Candice leaned back. "This is a celebration, so everyone, order what you want, our treat, and we'll get cupcakes to take home."

Back at the Phillips' house, after everyone had munched on cupcakes, then headed to their respective homes, Shayla printed off a packing list from the computer. She piled clothes on the bed; three pairs of capris and t-shirts, sandals, all of her underwear, three pairs of blue jeans and long-sleeved shirts, tennis shoes, warm weather pajamas, slippers, cold weather pajamas, three sweaters, two pairs of sweat pants, five pairs of wooly socks, a coat, her boots, makeup, hair dryer and hair brushes. *Whew, how am I going to get all of this in one suitcase?* She decided to trim it down to two capri and jean outfits, one sweater and one pair of sweats, that lightened the load a little, but it was still a lot of stuff, *I need help.* "Mom, how am I going to do this?"

Candice came into the room and chuckled. "I see your dilemma, I suggest you put the coat and boots on bottom, stuffing the wooly socks around the edge," she started the process, "then fold your sweats and sweaters in half with one at the top end and one at the bottom, meeting in the middle, next your winter PJ's, you can roll them like logs and place them around the back side, then the jeans and long-sleeved shirts will lie flat, placing the warm weather clothes, and jammies on top, after all that is done, place your underwear around the sides, with the cups of your bras folded into themselves and turned to the curved corners of the suitcase, like this." Mom straightened up and smiled. "I'll let you handle that and you should put each pair of extra shoes, in a bag to keep your clothes clean, then the shoe bags and hair dryer should go to the foot of the suitcase at the wheel end, to prevent as many wrinkles as possible, this way you can take your time unpacking and organizing you clothes in the closet by seasons."

Shayla surveyed the stack of clothes, folded her arms and stuck one foot out to the side, "Mom, do you think I need a passport?"

Candice laughed and swatted the air. "Don't be silly, Chick-a-dee and I've packed you a small bag of shampoo, face soap and moisturizer, you can put it in the outside zipper compartment," and left Shayla to the task.

Chapter 8

Thursday Morning

Up early the next morning, Shayla showered, fixed her hair and makeup, added the hair dryer to her suitcase, which she had to sit on to zip it closed, then stuck the shampoo pouch in the outside zipper. She placed her small makeup bag, two toothbrushes and toothpaste in her purse and checked her packing list again.

Mom walked into her room. "Your brothers should be here any minute, do you need any help, sweetie?"

"Morning Mom, only if you have a forklift, this bag weighs a ton."

Laughter filled the room. "So, you think you have

everything you need?"

She tugged at the suitcase handle. "According to the list I printed off last night, I have enough for me and half the girls on my floor."

Candice smiled. "Good for you, always be prepared and have enough to share."

"Thanks, but what I could use is a little extra sleep, whose idea was it to leave at five?"

The front door opened. "That must be the boys. Come on, I'll get your dad to put your bag in the car."

Shayla tugged the bag down the hall and into the dining room.

Rounding the corner in front of her daughter, Mom saw all of her flock; Ashton, Bailey, Mican, Maddy, and Max with his hands on his granddaughter's shoulders. Mom's head tipped to the side as she smiled. "Morning, Chick-a-dees."

Max responded, "Morning, Momma Hen."

Laughter filled the room, including Candice's.

Tom walked in. "What's so funny?"

A big old paw clapped onto his back. "You had to be there, Philly. Come on, let's get some grub."

Candice started to lead the way to the kitchen, but turned and asked, "Honey, will you put Shayla's suitcase in the car while I'm serving, but will you say the blessing first?"

Max looked at Tom. "Did she mean you or me as honey?" and Max's flashed his cheesy grin.

In his usual fashion, Tom smiled and touched his chest. "No, Max, I'm *honey*," then he added, "sure thing, sweetheart!"

Max patted his chest. "So, I'm sweetheart?"

Tom looked at the floor and shook his head. "Everyone, bow your heads for the blessing, please."

The family stopped in their tracks and took the hand of the person next to them.

"Dear Heavenly Father, thank you for this food we're about to eat and please watch over our children as they travel. Get them to their destination safely, foil all the plans and plots of the enemy along the way and bless Shayla on her new path, that I'm sure you've provided, in Jesus' name, amen."

Candice gave him a peck on the cheek. "Thank you, sweetie."

He grabbed Shayla's suitcase as the others filed into the kitchen.

Dishes and silverware clanked as Mom served scrambled eggs, grits, bacon and toast.

Shayla leaned over to give her a hug. "Mom, thank you for this great breakfast and for all of the love and support you've always given me."

Before Mom could answer, Max leaned in. "What about me, Sarge?"

Shayla laughed. "You too, Max," and gave him a kiss on the cheek. "I'm so glad God brought you and Philly into our lives. Even though our father was a wonderful man, I can't imagine life without you two in it. You've always been terrific to us." She glanced at Mican nuzzling Madelaine's ear. "I know Mican's grateful."

Max looked over and chuckled. "I couldn't have wished for a better husband for my Maddy. You know that girl fell in love with him the first time she met him and never changed her mind, not even an ounce." He looked at Candice and Shayla, "and I couldn't have wished for a better family for my granddaughter to be a part of." His eyes glistened with tears, but he cleared his throat. "Now stop stalling and let's eat."

Tom joined them and looked at Max as he and Shayla walked toward the table. "What's up with him?"

Candice handed her husband a plate. "Getting a little nostalgic and sentimental, I think."

Chapter 9

After Breakfast

The family walked to the car with Shayla, Ashton and Mican. Tom started the engine and it idled in the driveway. "Come on, you three, the road is waiting." He walked around to the other side.

Mican kissed Maddy goodbye.

Ashton hugged Bailey and nibbled on her neck as she giggled.

Mom held Shayla in a tight embrace. "Oh honey, I'm so excited for you to start this new adventure, but I'm going to miss you so much. I want you to have a wonderful time, I'm sure the Lord is in this, I don't know where it will lead, but I know you were meant for great things."

Wiping away her tears, "I love you so much, Mom and I'm going to miss you too!" Shayla reached to get a hug, "but it's only twenty weeks and I'll be back and I'll probably be stationed somewhere nearby." Tom walked up and she smiled. "You too, Philly Phillips, take care of your filly," she giggled.

He gave her a hug.

Max approached with a pack of cookies. "That's my cue for a hug, here's a snack for the road, I love you Sergeant Kitten Copper."

She wrapped her arms around his large frame. "Take care of everyone for me while I'm gone."

He pushed her to arm's length, but held onto her shoulders. "As always, my dear Kitten, as always."

Mican climbed behind the wheel, Shayla opened the front passenger door as Ashton squeezed into the back seat.

Shayla turned to her stepdad and Max. "What all did you guys pack in here? Ash barely has enough room to sit."

Max laughed. "Well, you'll need a mattress pad and a pillow, Quantico's beds are as hard as a rock."

Tom joined in. "And you'll need a heater and a fan, those are in the trunk with your suitcase. You can never tell what the temp will be like in the dorm. Besides that, you'll need a coffee pot, coffee, cups, filters, and clothes hangers, hopefully your roommate will bring a fridge, if not you can buy a small one in town and split the cost. Plus, Quantico 'll have a swap night, so Max and I gathered up some swag for you.[xiii] Oh, and I put your laptop in its bag and put it in a safe place, it's in the floor behind the drivers' seat."

Her eyebrows lifted. "What's swag?"

Max laughed. "Just local junk, like a cup from the Cookie Jar Café and your mug from the Sallis police station, we'll get you another one to replace it, some postcards of Tennessee and a poster advertising the Highway 127 Yard Sale."

"What? People like that stuff?"

"Oh, it's vital." Tom laughed. "It's memorabilia from the best twenty weeks of your life, now climb in." He pushed her toward the open door, she climbed in as ordered and he pushed it closed behind her. "Okay, Mican, get her on the road before she changes her mind."

Mican put the car in gear and edged forward, at the end of the driveway, he glanced to his left. "There's a strange dark car down the road with one guy sitting inside, I think he just ducked, so I couldn't see him, creepy, reminds me of when we found that underground base back there."[xiv]

Ashton leaned to see around the pile of stuff packed in beside him, but unsuccessfully. "Maybe someone's looking at buying the property."

Mican chuckled. "Yeah, right, at five o'clock in the morning and with a secret underground base for a basement." He turned onto the road placing Shayla on the side facing the porch.

Frantic waves and shouts of goodbye greet her ears.

With her arm out the open window, she waved, a tear rolling down her cheek. "What am I doing?"

Ashton leaned forward. "Shayla Marie, if Abba sent you through a portal to Quantico, would you question it?"

She snapped around to face him. "Of course not."

"Okay, then, consider this car a portal, it's just going to be a long, slow wormhole that gets you there." His sternness changed to a grin. "Honest, Shay, this is going to be the hardest work you've ever done, but the most rewarding. You were *asked* to come to Quantico. You were *invited.* That rarely *ever* happens. Do you know how special that is? How special you are?"

Her eyebrows knit together. "How do you know?"

He leaned back and laughed. "Max and Philly told me."

Chapter 10

Out of Cookies

Within the first hour of the drive, they ran out of cookies.

"Can we stop for something to eat? And I need to stretch my legs," Ashton's feet shuffled, "this back seat is cramped."

"Ash, I don't want to stop yet, this is a nice highway and I want to make good time while we can. Besides you just ate a large breakfast an hour ago."

"It doesn't matter. I'd like a snack." He leaned forward and pulled on the seat. "What about you, Shay? Wouldn't you like a second breakfast?"

She turned enough to see her brother's face and burst out laughing. "That looks suspiciously like Max's grin."

Laughter from Mican clinched it. "Well, that settles it. We'd stop for Max, so we'll stop for you, Ash. At the next fast food restaurant, we'll all take a bathroom break and get something to munch on."

Ashton leaned back. "Deal!"

Shayla glanced at her brothers. "Do you guys remember when we were little and Mom and Dad would take us on vacation?"

Mican lowered his voice. "Okay, you three, settle down back there, don't make me have to pull over."

Shayla leaned forward and giggled. "But Daddy, he touched me."

Ashton roared with laughter in the backseat. "I did it too, didn't I, just to make you whine?"

Mican's imitation voice roared. "Shay-Belle, don't be a Touch-Me-Not, all your petals will fall off."

Bursting with laughter, she leaned her head toward Mican's shoulder. "That was a perfect imitation," then she snapped up straight. "Oh, my, that's the first time I've really thought of Dad, since Tom and Max came into our lives. I should be ashamed of myself."

Ashton plopped his hands on the back of her seat again and pulled forward as far as his seatbelt would allow. "Don't be ridiculous, Shay. Dad loved us beyond measure, and he wouldn't want you to be sad and gloomy all the time and I'm sure he would approve of Tom and Max. They came into our lives and rescued us and Mom.[xv] They're a blessing and Dad would want us to be blessed! So, stop that negative thinking and besides, I think he'd be proud of you for going to Quantico. We don't know what kind of training he had because his file is classified, but I'm sure he'd be proud."

Shayla's mouth dropped open, and her eyebrows reached for her hairline. "Ashton, I'm surprised at you!"

His eyes responded by opening wider. "Why? Do you think I'm wrong?"

She couldn't hold the stunned look any longer and burst out giggling. "No, because I think you're right for a change."

He leaned back and folded his arms. "Very

funny, sis, very funny."

Mican replied in Dad's voice. "Don't be pouty, Ashton, you know you're loved."

A pucker of his lips accompanied, "You're very funny too, bro."

Shayla pointed. "Look, Mican, there's a food place."

Mican glanced at this brother in the rearview mirror. "We can swop places too, if you like."

Ashton grinned. "I think you should take Shay's seat and she should rotate back here." He leaned forward. "Not so funny now, is it, Shay-smell?"

Her eyes popped open wide. "Shay-smell?" She turned to look at him, "now there's a blast from the past." They all burst out laughing.

Chapter 11

Eleven Hours Later

After a long day, they drove onto the base. "Oh, my goodness, we're finally here." Shayla stepped from the car and stretched. "It took eleven hours, but the last two were fighting D.C. and Manassas traffic."

Mican stepped from the backseat. "Not like Sallis, eh, Copper?"

Her face reflected a mischievous smile. "Only during the Highway 127 Yard Sale, then our dinky little town becomes a zoo."

Ashton emerged from the driver's seat. "That's the truth, one weekend out of the year Sallis feels like a big town." He tapped his watch, "and Shay, don't forget the time is an hour ahead here. It's getting late."

Shayla looked around. "I'd better check in."

"This way, mademoiselle." Mican swished his hand toward a nearby building.

She narrowed her eyes. "How do you know?"

He pointed up. "It says Administration Building right above the door."

They strolled the sidewalk and up the steps.

Ashton held the door as Shayla entered, followed by Mican.

They were greeted at the desk by a woman in uniform. "Special Agent McKnight, how good to see you. I see you've brought the other Special Agent McKnight with you and a new person. Ahh, who have we here?"

Mican nodded. "Good evening, Agent Timmens, this is our sister Shayla McKnight."

Shayla looked side-to-side. "Special Agents? You two are Special Agents of the FBI?"

Ashton laughed. "Not your ordinary Special Agents, Shay. Mican is in Antiquities Theft

Recovery and I'm in Research and Development."

"But Mican's an archeologist, he's been interested in it since archeology camp when he was fifteen and we,"[xvi] she stopped abruptly. "So, what are you researching and developing, Ash?"

He stared at the floor, then looked up again. "I can't tell you here, sis, Agent Timmens doesn't have a high enough clearance to know."

Shayla ducked her chin. "No, way!"

Ashton nodded. "Yes, way, is all I can say."

Looking from her brothers to Timmens, Shayla placed her hands on her hips "So why are you guys Special Agents and Timmens is just an Agent? Is it because she's a woman?"

Timmens responded with a smile, "No, it's because an Agent is a federal law enforcement officer with arrest authority, but who doesn't usually conduct major criminal investigations.[xvii] It's not a lesser position, just a different designation for clarity."

Mican poked his sister in the back and laughed. "We'll tell you more later. Come on, we're supposed to meet Max."

Her hands flew up. "Max?"

"Yeah, he's choppering up to meet us and fly Ashton and me back home."

"But why didn't he just fly us up here?"

Ashton responded. "Because, goose, you'll need your car." He turned to face the person at the desk. "Timmens will you check the paperwork and be sure we brought the right person."

She chuckled. "If she's Shayla Marie McKnight, she's the right person, and a very special one it seems. She was requested by powers that be," she turned her head a little, "to attend FBI School at The Big Q." She glanced at Shayla. "Oooo, not just anybody gets in here and to be requested, well that's a one-in-a-million. Congratulations, Miss McKnight."

Shayla looked at Ashton with one eyebrow cocked, then turned to the desk. "It's nice to meet you, Agent Timmens, please call me Shayla or Shay for short."

Following the assignment of a dorm room and the signing of some paperwork, she received a couple of uniforms, an exercise outfit, a jogging suit, a leaflet with information and a class schedule. "Your brothers will show you where to go and good luck, Shay."

Mican took her by the elbow. "Come on, trainee, we'll help you unload the car and then we'll meet Max for dinner. He just texted that he'll arrive in twenty minutes. We've gotta hustle."

He pulled the car to the entrance of the dorm, when the last load, arrived in the room, Shayla forced out a rush of air. "Thank goodness, that's done and thanks for your help, bubbas, I think dad and Max overdid things."

Ashton looked around. "Man, this brings back memories and no, I think you'll be surprised that you'll need every single thing they packed for you, they're pros, remember."

She plopped her fists on her waist. "No wonder you two knew so much about what I would go through, so when did you guys come here?"

Ashton pointed at Mican. "He came first, before he got married four years ago, then I came the next year right after Bailey and I got hitched."

Shayla puckered her lips before speaking. "How come I didn't know when you guys attended Quantico?"

Ashton lifted his shoulders. "Well, I guess you're not very bright."

Mican laughed. "Stop it, Ash." Then turned to his sister. "We had to keep it a secret, Shay, even Maddy didn't know. She thought I was on a dig in Israel, but really, I was here training. I wasn't able to tell her until after we got married, not before. You were busy with your training at the Police Academy, so you didn't question it when I left."

She folded her arms. "So, when did you know that you wanted to work in antiquity theft recovery?"

"When I was at the beginning of my doctoral work, I went to the Middle East with a school group, remember?"

"Yes, I remember. So, that was a real school trip?

And you really are an archeologist, right?"

He folded his arms. "Yes, it was real and on our way home, one of the customs agents told Professor Dodds that they were being extra careful when people came back from the Middle East because they were having so many artifacts looted. The customs agent listed a number of treasures that they knew for sure had been stolen. The Professor talked to us on the flight home about being ethical in our work. Anyone who was after monetary rewards had better think twice because prison time would be in the country of origin of any artifact stolen and they were not like American prisons. He gave such a compelling speech that I decided then and there that the two things I wanted to do most in my work were, to do research and to recover artifacts. I told Professor Dodds, so when he was approached and asked whether he knew anyone who would be interested in applying to the Antiquities Theft Division, the professor mentioned my name and put in a good word for me. I was thrilled and when I finished my PhD in May, I applied straight to

Quantico, I was accepted that summer and started in August, like you're doing."

Shayla sat down on the edge of her bunk. "So, you've kept this from me for four years and I never suspected. I'm not much of a copper, am I?"

Mican chuckled. "No, you're more of a kitten than a copper."

Her mouth pulled to one side as she punched him on the upper arm. "I'm a what?"

He grabbed the top of his arm. "Ouch! You're a Sergeant Copper, ma'am."

All three laughed.

She scowled at her other brother and folded her arms. "Now what about you, Ash-booger?"

"Ash-booger! Oooo, I like it, it reminds me of the old days."[xviii]

Shayla unfolded her arms and patted the bed for her brothers to sit with her. "Seriously Ash, what do you do and how did you get into it?"

"Similar to Mican, I got interested in college while getting my Masters' degree in engineering. I talked to Philly and Max about what I could do for a career. Everything seemed so bland until I started to talk about our time travel experiences through portals when we were teens.[xix] That brought up a conversation about Abba using mirrors and windows to move you, Shay and some of those kids you rescued the day Mom and Philly got married.[xx] Max had heard of a new research program studying," he made air quotation marks, "The Possibility of Time Travel and/or Movement through Space, Via Portals or Transit Points," he let out air, "whew!" "This project came out of one of the quantum physics studies they'd been doing. Anyway, I applied and was accepted, but," he laughed, "I'm probably the only person on the project who has actually time traveled."

Shayla tucked her chin. "So, you're not a lepidopterist at the Butterfly Exhibit at the zoo?"

"Well, of course I am," he winked. "Patrice[xxi] and her 'herd' of butterflies got me interested in studying Lepidoptera, and I study a lot of other things too, like how Abba might have done what he did moving us into Old Testament times," he laughed, "but I don't dare tell any of my co-workers about our experience."

She tipped her head. "Why not?"

"Duh, do you want them to think I'm a loon?"

Folding one arm across her body and placing her thumb under her chin with her index finger to the side of her face, she replied. "You don't have to tell them, just ask who's been on a time travel adventure. Say it in a joking manner, the ones who stare at the floor, probably have been, the workers who laugh, probably haven't, then over time talk to the people who stared at the floor. Bring up Abba as a kick-starter to the conversation."

Mican's phone chirped. "Max wants to know where we are. He's hungry!"

Shayla rolled her eyes and smiled. "As usual."

Chapter 12

Dinner with Max

A short walk brought them to the front entrance of The Clubs. Max waved as they approached. "Hurry up, you three, they close at seven and I want some of the Mongolian BBQ. It's only eighty-eight cents an ounce tonight.[xxii] My treat, but get in there."

Shayla giggled as she walked past. "They don't know what they're in for tonight, do they, Uncle Max?"

Seated at a table, Shayla told Max what the boys had shared with her.

"Yeah, Kitten, it's becoming quite a family

tradition. I wouldn't be a bit surprised if your birth-dad, hadn't attended here at some point, then Tommy-Boy and I …"

Shayla shook her head. "You sure do have a lot of nicknames for dad, Tommy-Boy, Philly, Tom."

He winked. "It's all part of the fun, Kitten, you know, code names. Anyway, Tommy-Boy and I both passed through here, but in different decades." He grinned. "In fact, we met on a mission and we've been best friends ever since. When Tom was trying to help your mom, after she lost your dad, I was the person he called, but even before I met Candice, I had heard her story and I knew she and Tom were meant for each other. Over the phone, I could tell by the way he talked about her that he was smitten. Of course, she took a little more convincing." Laughter erupted causing heads to turn his direction. "It took him four years for Philly Phillips to lasso that filly." Another chuckle. "Philly and his filly, that boy cracks me up."

Shayla laughed. "Yeah, their wedding day, you both looked as nervous as two long-tailed cats in a room full of rocking chairs."

Laughter burst out again. "I think Tommy-Boy was afraid she wouldn't show up. I was afraid he'd pass out if she didn't. Little did we know, at that moment, you were jetting all over the country rescuing kids."[xxiii]

Slumping in her seat, Shayla said, "I was afraid I was going to miss the wedding, but Abba is so faithful. I looked a mess when I got back, but Bailey switched clothes with me and fixed my hair and makeup in a flash. That girl's a true artist."

Ashton sighed. "I wish she'd be that fast at home."

Max turned his head toward Ashton. "Ash, you know Abba's done a fine work in that girl."

He lifted his arms. "Yeah, but I had to wait twelve years for her to get saved and grow in the Lord before I could marry her, I loved her all that time, but I couldn't tell her."

Shayla smiled. "That must have been really hard Ash, but now she's a treasure," she glanced to Mican and Max, "like Madelaine, now I have the two best sisters-in-law in the world, as different as night and day, I might add, but both are splendid."

Max's eyes beamed as he scanned the faces before him. "Now eat up, you scalawags! They'll be closing this place in a few minutes."

On the tarmac, the hot August night and the steamy asphalt assisted the helicopter's engine to warm up faster than normal.

Mican glanced into the cockpit as Max ran through his pre-flight checklist, then turned back to his sister. "He'll be finished any minute, sis, we'd better climb onboard."

Shayla hugged each of her brothers before they ducked below the rotor blades and entered the chopper. Backing away, Shayla waved goodbye as Max pulled up on the cyclic collective like she'd seen him do so many times before.

The copter lifted him and her two brothers into the air.

In a moment she stood alone. *Abba, what have I done? Are you sure this is where you want me to be?*

I feel so empty standing here. I've left a job I loved, friends I loved, my mom, Philly and all of my family that I love. She smiled, but a tear ran down her cheek. *Even our lovely grizzly bear, Max isn't with me.*

Out of the darkness a voice shook her back to the moment. "Hey you! What are you doing out here?"

Her head and body spun almost involuntarily. "Huh, I'm, I mean, I just said goodbye to my family."

He marched up to within inches of her face. "This is a restricted area, no unaccompanied civilians allowed."

Stammering, she tried to explain. "I was accompanied, but all of them flew away just before you came up. How am I going to get back to my room if I can't go unaccompanied?"

His voice softened. "So, you're a trainee? I'll have to verify your story. Come with me." He took her elbow in a clinch and led her to his jeep.

Out of the corner of her eye, Shayla saw the silhouette of a man in the shadows. "Who's he? He's unaccompanied."

"Don't worry about him, he has credentials up to

his eyeballs. He's the one who pointed you out to me."

She sniffed as she climbed into the jeep. "Nosey busybody."

When they arrived at the Administration Building, the security officer took her elbow again and led her to the door and opened it.

Timmens laughed. "Are you in trouble already, Shayla? You really are a McKnight, aren't you?"

The guard loosened his grip on her arm. "Agent Timmens, you know this person?"

"Yes, Jager, and you will too before long." As her head tipped back, a gentle laugh flowed from her lips. "She's bound to be trouble, so many people in her family have been through here, she should have inherited a spot, but it seems she's a special one. She was invited to attend."

"You mean, recruited?"

Timmens shook her head. "Nope, she had received backing and was asked to come."

"Wow, invited, I didn't even know that could happen. I had to work hard for my spot."

The agent leaned onto the desk. "I'm sure she did too, we just aren't privy to what she's done, but I assure you, this one," she pointed at Shayla, "is special. There are at least three different agencies that requested she receive an invitation to Quantico."

Jager turned to Shayla. "I'm sorry, ma'am, I hope I didn't hurt your arm. How can I make it up to you?"

A red elbow tilted upwards as she rubbed it. "Don't worry, I'm fine, but if you *really* want to make it up to me, you can show me how to get back to my room. I got here this evening and my brothers were leading the way. I was so blown away by the fact that they were both Special Agents, I guess I didn't pay enough attention."

Timmens pushed a paper at him with the room assignment. "Shayla, I know you only received your invitation three days ago, so you'll need to review the information I gave you this afternoon, it has your class schedule and a map in it. Remember, classes start bright and early Monday morning, so get yourself settled and acclimated quickly."

Jager led the way out of the building and down

the steps. "Do you think your brothers' agencies were two of the three that requested you receive an invitation?"

"I doubt it, they were surprised when I told them I had been invited and I'm sure they would have told me after we arrived. They insisted on helping me drive here from Tennessee, but they didn't tell me they were agents until we got here, the sneaky boogers."

He laughed. "Sneaky boogers, is that Tennessee talk?"

She felt her face flash hot. "I guess it is. I've lived there since I was thirteen."

His eyes cut her direction. "And how many years has that been?"

They reached the dorm and the realization that he might be flirting with her, caught her off-guard. She lifted one eyebrow and turned to face him. "More than you can count, mister." She reached for the door handle, tugged and smiled. "Thanks for showing me back safely, Security Officer Jager," and she slipped inside.

Chapter 13

First Night

Back in the room, the task of unpacking overwhelmed her, tired from getting up at four, plus the long road trip, though it was only eight o'clock Tennessee time, she pulled out the mattress pad and pillow, piled them on one of the two beds, pulled a sheet up over herself and prayed. "Abba, bless Mican, Ashton and Max for helping me get here. I'm sure they're home by now, so give them and all my family a good night's rest and thank you for this opportunity, help me to make the most of my time here, show me your direction for my life, and fill this lonely, empty feeling inside me, in Jesus' name, amen." Her eyes closed and she fell fast asleep.

Back in Tennessee, Tom Phillips waited

at the Sallis Airfield. When the helicopter arrived his two stepsons jumped from their seats, ducked beneath the rotor blades and headed his direction, while Max secured the chopper.

"I had to beat the women off of me to get here." Tom chuckled. "Seems your wives are anxious to see you. Crawl in the back seat, we'll let Max sit up front."

When they opened the rear doors, the overhead light came on, Maddy and Bailey sat up.

Mican shouted, "What are you doing here?"

Maddy rubbed her belly. "The baby and I couldn't wait to see you."

Bailey laughed and rubbed her belly. "Yeah, the baby and I couldn't wait to see you either."

"Knock it off, Bailey, you're not ..." His eyebrows rose. "Are you?"

Maddy and Bailey looked at each other and giggled, then looked back at their husbands.

Tom observed the whole interaction in the

rearview mirror. "Yep, Ash, Bailey looked at the test stick after you left, but wanted to tell you this evening, in person, when you got home. Your mom and I are thrilled. By the way, you can close your mouth now."

Mican and the girls laughed.

Ashton's lower jaw remained sagged open, then his face lit up. "I'm thrilled. Are you thrilled? Of course, you are. We talked about wanting a baby months ago. I'm just in shock that's all."

Max jogged up. "What'd I miss?"

A radiant face drew his attention. "I'm going to have a baby, Uncle Max, you're going to be a great uncle."

"I'm gonna to be a what?"

Bailey repeated. "A great grandpa for Maddy and Mican's baby and a great uncle for our baby, so I think we should call you a grandpa-uncle or grand puncle."

He grinned. "You can call me whatever you like, as long as you let me babysit the little rascal."

Chapter 14

First Day on Her Own

Shayla awoke and stretched. *Hmm, six o'clock, is that Tennessee time or here?* Still dressed in her travel clothes from yesterday, complete with shoes, she cracked her dorm room door and peeked at the clock at the end of the hall. *Okay, I have to reset my watch,* she looked at her phone, *duh, or use my cell phone for time. It's seven o'clock Eastern, I wonder what I can get to eat.* Pulling out the instructions Timmens had given her she looked under the headings for food. *The canteen is open for breakfast until eight*, she looked at the map, *I don't* *have time to change if I'm going to get something to eat.* She looked in the mirror and groaned. "Yuck." She pushed her hair back behind her ears, put on her sunglasses, grabbed her purse and dashed.

Right outside the dorm, she ran into Jager, right where he'd left her last night. "Aren't those the same duds you were wearing yesterday, McKnight?" He laughed.

"What are you doing here? I fell asleep in my clothes and just woke up. I'm trying to get to the canteen to get something to eat before it closes."

"I just got off shift and I need to return the jeep to the vehicle compound which happens to be right behind to the Canteen. Hop in and I'll get you there in plenty of time before it closes."

Her voice came out snarly, "Oh, all right, thanks, Jager."

"Are you always this grumpy in the mornings?" She climbed into the idling jeep and Jager pulled into a main lane and headed south.

"Not that it's any of your business, but my body hasn't adjusted to the new Time Zone and I feel out-of-sorts, leaving my family, my job and my friends behind. I don't know anyone here and I have to learn my way around before Monday, I was too tired to unpack last night and I don't even know where to start with that."

"I can understand, let's start by getting you some breakfast and see if that won't make you feel better. By the way," he pointed to her right, "that's the building where all the new trainees' basic classes are held," he pointed again across the street, "there's the regular cafeteria," he slowed down and pointed down a side street, "what they call Hogan's Alley is straight down there. That's where most of your physical activities and field workshops will be held."

She nodded. "Thanks, Jager, that's an enormous help."

The jeep stopped in front of the Canteen, as she climbed out and headed to the door, Jager called out, "do you want me to join you for breakfast?"

"No, but thanks for the lift."

Louder, "Do you want me to help you unpack?"

"No thanks, Jager, you've been a great help

already," and the door closed behind her.

Chapter 15

First Day of Classes

Following a detailed orientation, Shayla's first class was on 'Tailing a Suspect,' at the conclusion of the lecture portion, the class met at the entrance of Hogan's Alley.

Huh! I expected this to be a rundown industrial area, but look, it has a bank, theater, nice corner building, and all kinds of shops. I'm sure I'll see all of those before it's over.

"McKnight! Daydream on your own time!"

"Sorry, Sir!"

In a loud droning voice, the instructor bellowed, his voice hitting a higher pitch emphasizing the last word. "Your first assignment is in *surveillance*. You will either trail or be *trailed*. Each team will be given maps of the route they are expected to take, to get a *point*, you must arrive back at this *spot*," he pointed at a circle in front of his feet, "without being marked by your opponent with this type of *pen*," the instructor held up an implement, "if you get *marked*, the one trailing you gets the *point*. Your first time out, will be a short route, as you become more experienced, the routes will lengthen. Keep in mind, this is not a speed drill, it's a test of your cunning and ability to stay out of sight or a test of your ability to surveil a person who does not want to be *followed*. One catch though, the person being followed cannot go *inside* a building neither can they get *inside* a vehicle, parked or moving. You must use your wits to avoid being *marked*, do you understand?"

The class shouted. "Yes, Sir!"

"Here are the teams and the assignments."

"Jefferson and Todds, McKnight and Silas …"

He handed Shayla a paper with a route map. *I'm the one to be followed.*

"We will begin the exercise on my *mark*, Jefferson and Todds, line up *here*. Jefferson, you are the suspect being tailed, you will have a ten second *head start*. You *must* stick to your route, you cannot *deviate*." The instructor looked at a stop watch. "Jefferson, go!"

The instructor turned to Shayla. "McKnight, you and Gordan Silas are the next pair, we will give the first team a five-minute lead, we don't want you trainees getting caught-up in someone else's exercise.

Shayla studied her route map, true to his word, five minutes on the nose.

"McKnight, on the line. Go!"

Taking off across the road and to the right of the corner building, Shayla new she needed to make it to the turn before Silas took off. *Oh, I wish I had taken this jacket off before I started.* She reached the first corner, but of course, Silas with his long legs was on the move and saw her turn. *I have to find cover.* She scanned the area, to the left, stood a flower stall, *nah, he'll check every flower and under every basket*, so instead, she crossed the street to the ladies clothing store, grabbed a large dress and shawl from a sale rack on the sidewalk, she pulled the dress over her head, tugged it down over her clothes, leaving her hair tucked inside the collar and stuffed the shawl underneath the dress, against her backside and bending slightly, she waddled down the street in full view.

While the flower vendor gave Silas fits for messing up her display, Shayla snuck around the next corner. *No sight of Silas. Abba, what am I to do?* She yanked off the dress and shawl dropping them in the gutter and darted to her next location. At the furniture store, she noticed movers loading a van. *I know I can't get inside,* she panted, looked around and dashed to the far side of the truck just as Gordon Silas rounded the corner.

She stepped onto the runner of the truck and pulled herself up, climbed using the open window of the cab for a foothold and made it to the roof, *ouch, wowee, hot, hot, hot! I'm glad I have on these long sleeves now Abba, thanks,* she tugged the sleeves over her fists and on her hands and knees, she peaked over the ledge.

Her opponent headed toward the truck.

She inched back and flattened onto the roof, but heard his movements, she could tell he rummaged inside the back, then he opened the cab and looked inside.

That's not nice, he thinks I would cheat! She peeked over the front of the truck and watched as Gordon turned and dashed around the corner, shaking his head. With his back to her, she slid off the truck on the far side, placed her foot on the window sill, then onto the running board, she stepped down, dropped to her knees and watched from underneath the truck.

Silas lit out down the side street.

Shayla had become the one trailing, she scrunched down and crept to the corner.

Silas raced to the next turn on the map. He looked behind trash cans and in discarded boxes, but something behind her made a noise and he turned.

She barely escaped detection by ducking into a

doorway, but the boxes gave her an idea. When Silas frantically made the next corner, Shayla ran to the boxes and chose a big one, she flipped it over her head, squatted, took her knife from her pocket and made small eyeholes. She crept to the corner, still under the box, ducked behind a trash can, scooted out to peer around the edge and waited for his next move, once her opponent moved, she lifted the box and dashed to the turn, lowering the box again, she eased around the corner, facing the last street.

Gordan Silas stood at the final corner before the return across the grass to the instructor, he scratched his head and looked both ways then scanned back the way he'd come without noticing the box. He finally stepped onto the walkway that crossed the field.

Shayla lifted the box, dashed down the sidewalk and squatted again under her covering at the spot where he'd lingered.

He walked toward the instructor with his hands on his hips and head down.

She lifted the box and dashed across the street, but when she squatted on the edge of the grass, she found she couldn't move the box. *What's going on? It's just a box!* It was as if a weight was sitting on top of it, dizziness spun in her head. She could feel a struggle outside, *is Gordan trying to lift my cover?* But she couldn't see anything through the peepholes. All of a sudden, as if the weight had been removed, the box lifted supernaturally, she glanced to the side and saw a dark shadow and a white streak, like smoke being blown away rapidly. Without making a sound she removed the box from her body, lowered it to the grass and sped down the path. Knowing Silas was left handed, she darted to his right, he turned, but to the left as expected, he saw her out of the corner of his eye as she zipped past him and scrambled to the safety spot in front of the instructor.

Jumping up and down, she shouted, "Yahoo!"

Silas flapped his arms.

She watched as the instructor put a one-point stroke next to her name. "Good work, McKnight. I thought for a minute there you weren't going to come out from under that box, but you made it. Where'd you learn to run so fast and evade detection like that?"

"Playing Hide and Seek, sir! I have two older brothers, sir."

The instructor chuckled. "Join the other trainees on the bleachers."

Chapter 16

The Window

At his workstation, Ashton sat staring at a contraption he made. His pencil kept beat to the tick-tick-tick of a timer. A mirror, lying flat, reflected the overhead light and electrical arms extended like octopus tentacles from the frame. The sudden *ding-a-ling-a-ling* of an alarm caused him to jump. He swatted the off button and noticed the face of the mirror becoming cloudy, he leaned in for a better look. The cloud began to spin and make a whooshing noise.

Coworkers heard the sound and began to gather around his station.

Someone shouted, "Get the camera!"

Feet shuffled and a guy with a camera ran up next to Ashton, nearly edging him out of his chair. The fog cleared and like a motion picture, a young woman appeared in the frame. A sinister shadow lurked behind her.

As the camera captured the event, Ashton leaned behind its operator. "Can you see the dark shadow behind her?"

"What dark shadow, Ash? All I see is this really pretty lady."

He scanned the faces of the others. "Can anyone see a dark shadow?"

One-by-one the answer came. "No, Ash."

Ashton dashed from the room, pulled his phone from his pocket and dialed. "Mican, I've created a window."

"Good for you, bro." Mican chuckled.

"No, doofus! I can see Shay. She's in danger. There's a dark shadow creeping up on her, but none of my coworkers can see the shadowy figure, they only see Shayla. I think Abba's giving us a warning."

Mican's voice changed. "Let me step out into the

hall." A door creaked and shut hard behind him. "Abba, Ash and I believe you are giving us a warning about danger approaching Shayla. Heavenly Father, we thank you for this warning and for your protection. We ask you to send," his voice rose, "no — *launch* — your warring angels to Shayla's aid, *now*, Father, in Jesus' name, amen."

A burst of air rushed from Ashton. "Bro, I feel peace starting to cover me."

"Me too, Ash, thanks for calling and I appreciate that you didn't take this lightly. Your growth in spiritual warfare is amazing. I'm proud of you, bro."

"Thanks, Mican, but as usual, you were the cooler head. I was on the verge of panicking, when I saw that dark figure coming up behind Shayla, it creeped me out." He chuckled. "I'd better run, I have some *splaining* to do in the lab." He rushed to the restroom and threw a dab of water on his face and smeared it with his hand. When he reentered the lab, all eyes shot toward him.

"Dude, you missed it." The camera operator was still filming.

Ashton frantically asked, "Missed what?"

Across the table, Sadie said, "That girl in the mirror, just threw this really big guy over her head. He crept up behind her and grabbed her shoulder, she grabbed his wrist, dropped to one knee and he sailed over her head like a kite. It was awesome!"

He wiped more water from his face.

Another coworker asked, "What were you saying about a shadow following her? You rushed out of the room and when we looked back we saw the big guy sneaking up on her. How did you know?"

"I thought my eyes were playing tricks on me, so I went to splash some water on my face."

At that moment the mirror became cloudy again and the young woman disappeared.

The guy with the camera moaned. "Ahhh, man, bring her back Ash, she was pretty."

The cloud began to spin again, as it cleared, Ashton saw Mican standing before a group of men seated at a semicircular table. He spoke, but no audio accompanied the picture. A dark cloud moved into the frame and rested on the head of each man. "Uh-oh! Do you guys see that?"

The girl across from him lifted her eyes. "See what, Ashton?"

He cleared his throat. "Oh, nothing. I think I need more water on my face." He ran into the hall again. "Abba, what's going on. Is Mican in danger?"

He felt an urging to pray, in his spirit.

"Dear Father, thank you for what you're showing me, even if I don't completely understand it. I ask that you send your angels to remove the darkness from the room Mican is in, keep him safe and bless him in whatever he's trying to accomplish. May your will be done, in Jesus' name, amen!" Ashton raced back into the lab in time to see blobs of darkness lift from every man except one. The man covered with darkness stood and walked to the door, when he opened it and walked out of the room, all the other blobs of darkness followed him. In the image, Ashton watched as Mican smiled and walked around the interior of the semicircle and shook hands with each man in turn, then the image faded.

The director of the lab entered the room. "Why is

everyone gathered around Ashton's station?"

"Sir, you've got to see this." The technician rewound the camera and held it up.

"What am I supposed to be seeing, Jenkins?"

The technician turned the camera toward himself and all that was visible was static. "But sir, we all saw it!"

A stern voice responded, "Saw what? A whole bunch of you wasting time, visiting."

The female technician, Sadie chimed in. "No, sir, Ashton opened some kind of portal with this mirror," she pointed to the table, "we all saw two different scenes, one with a young woman in a gymnasium somewhere and one at a business meeting."

The director placed his hands on his waist. "McKnight is that true?"

"Yes, sir, but for some reason the camera didn't capture it."

"Very well, try to replicate what happened and call me next time. Now everyone back to your stations."

They all nodded, but when Dr. Clarence returned

to his office, Ashton slipped into the hallway again, pushed speed dial and Mican answered.

"Everything okay, Ash?"

"Yeah, but this was crazy. When I went back into the lab, the people were pointing to my gizmo and said Shayla threw a guy over her shoulder, then the picture cleared and you appeared in front of a semicircular table."

"Yeah, that's right, I was requesting an endowment from a corporation to fund my project in the Middle East. Why?"

"There were clouds over every persons' head until I prayed, then all the clouds lifted except for one. That man got up and left the room, taking all of the clouds with him."

"Hmmm, yep, that pretty much describes how it felt. That one guy was very negative and cynical, when he stormed out, the whole room looked brighter and felt more pleasant. Thanks for the prayers, Ash, I really appreciate it, I got the funding I was seeking."

"You're welcome, bro, but can we meet? I need

to talk to you."

"Sure, will the cafe at the end of Warner Park be okay?"

"That'll be great, I'll meet you there after work."

Chapter 17

Funding Secured

Mican returned to his office, pumped with excitement, he hung up his jacket and stepped next door and knocked.

"Come in!"

Grinning ear-to-ear, Mican announced, "Professor Dodds, I got the funding from the Cyber Tech Company."

Dodds leaned back in his chair. "Congratulations, my boy! This secures your place in studying the Copper Scroll. Good work, indeed. We'll schedule your flight immediately."

Mican's shoulders dropped. "But sir, our baby is due soon, can't I postpone until after the first of the year? I don't want to leave my wife alone now or right after the baby is born."

His boss took on a dark countenance. "We have to move now, son, we can't waste time because of sentimental family issues. I'll have to see if I can get Marks to take your place if you don't want to go."

"But sir! I want to go, I just …"

The professor looked across the desk at him. "Mican, maybe you can catch the next project."

"But, sir, can't …"

Dodds picked up the phone. "Sarah, get me John Marks."

Chapter 18

Two Minutes Past Four

Ashton came out of a store and crossed the street to the park. He dashed to the café to be greeted by his brother holding two cups of hot chocolate. "Thanks, dude, that'll be good now that the weather's getting chilly. Can we walk in the park and talk, I don't want our conversation to be overheard?"

"Sure thing, Ash, lead the way."

As they stepped onto the grass, Ashton began sharing. "I was working off of the idea of some of the things Shayla had told me about her being teleported through mirrors when she rescued those kids, so I was building a contraption of that sort when it suddenly activated."

Mican stopped to face him. "That's when you

saw the shadow sneaking up on Shay and called me, right?"

"Yeah, after you prayed and I went back in the room, they were telling me that Shayla flung some big guy over her shoulder, I didn't tell them she was my sister."

Mican chuckled. "Good for our little sis, being able to hoist some guy over her shoulder."

"The thing is, when it cleared, that's when I saw you, then the project manager came in and one of the guys had filmed the two events, but when he tried to replay them, it was all static."

"Hmmm! and?"

Ashton took a sip before continuing. "No one, but me, saw the shadows in either picture! I think Abba was orchestrating the pictures and I didn't have anything to do with it."

Mican stared at the ground and shook his head. "That must be disappointing for you, Ash, I'm sorry. I know how you feel, I had a major disappointment today too."

"What happened?"

"After the successful meeting, I went to see Dr. Dodds. The funding I received was enough to set me up on the project for six months, my boss was pleased, but wanted to send me to Jordan immediately. I reminded him that the baby was due soon, but he seemed so indifferent, so insensitive, not like himself at all. He was adamant that someone needed to go now, so he's going to send John Marks in my place."

"That's the job in Amman, right?"

Mican leaned in close. "Yeah, it's the Copper Scroll I was telling you about."

Ashton jerked back and shouted. "But that's your project! He can't do that. You were invited and you raised the funds, that's just not right!"

"Well he can and he is."

"We'll see about that!" Ashton reached for Mican's shoulder. "Abba, you know Mican's heart, you know that he's worked hard to get the funding to make this possible," his tone softened, "you know … but Father if it's not your will for Mican to go to Jordan and to work on the Copper Scroll Project, we accept that, but if it is for Mican to have this project, make it so, Lord. We place it in your hands. Forgive me for my anger and forgive Mican for his disappointment. We want your will to be done, Father, in the name of your son, amen." He turned to his brother. "We'll have to wait and see what Abba does."

At that moment, the ground trembled as if a T-rex approached, knowing they weren't far from the zoo, Mican and Ashton both glanced around for an elephant or something charging at them, but Mican's eyes were drawn to a puddle next to where they stood. Ripples on the water's surface caused by the tremor, faded and the water became cloudy. Mican pointed. "Uh, oh, Ash, look."

Glancing at the puddle, Ashton and Mican both saw their sister again with a large man running toward her from behind, a dark shadow lurked nearby.

Without a second thought, Ashton dropped to one knee beside the puddle and shouted, "Look out, Shay!"

Her image turned, as if she heard his warning.

Mican shouted, "No weapon formed against our sister will prosper."

In the image, they saw Shayla turn, her hands grabbed the man's shirt at his shoulders, she leaned back and her bottom sank to the ground, pulling her attacker off balance, her feet stomped into the man's abdomen, she rolled back and tossed him over her head. A Security Officer ran toward the guy on the ground and jerked a knife from his hand.

Shayla jumped to her feet, her hands flew to a defensive position and she faced the direction of the man sprawled on the ground, this time audio accompanied the picture. "Jager, where'd you come from?"

The Security Officer used his walkie to call for back up, before approaching Shayla, "I saw you walking across campus and was going to try to ask you out again, but," he chuckled, "now I'm not so sure I want to."

"Ha, ha, very funny, Jager."

He pointed to the attacker. "Who's this guy,

McKnight and why was he after you? Did he try to ask you out and you turned him down too?"

She propped her fists on her hips. "You're very funny, but to answer your question, I guess I embarrassed him in Self-Defense class this morning. I threw him over my shoulder."

Help arrived and the Security Officer pointed to the body on the ground. "Take him into custody for Assault with a Deadly Weapon." He held the knife at the end with his fingertips, bagged it and handed it to a security guard, "log this," and turned back to Shayla. "Seriously, are you okay?"

Shayla rubbed her lower back. "Yeah, I'm fine, my back should be hurting from his weight, but it's not. I guess he's lighter than he looks."

Jager watched as the security team tried to cuff him and get him to his feet. "That would be a *no*, McKnight, he's not light." He turned back to face Shayla. "You won't have any more trouble out of him, I witnessed the whole event and he'll go to prison for a few years since this happened on Federal land, then he'll be kicked out. His career with any government agency is over permanently."

With a grimace, she remarked, "Oh, great, I hope he doesn't know my name."

He smiled and said, "You could always get married and change it."

She tilted her head. "Can't we just be friends? I've been sent here on a mission and I don't have time for anything else."

His sideways glance caught her attention. "Mission?"

"I mean, I've been tapped or should I say, recommended by three different agencies and I don't even know why, for sure, or who instigated it, so I have to take this seriously."

He saluted. "Yes ma'am, Serious Trainee, McKnight. May I escort you to your dorm again?"

Smiling she shook her head, no. "I think I've got it now, Jager, but thanks for coming to my rescue."

He turned his head slightly. "Don't you mean for coming to *his* rescue?" He laughed, as he turned and walked away.

The water at Mican and Ashton's feet clouded

and returned to a normal puddle.

"See Mican, Abba's doing this. How can I explain this to my project manager?"

"I don't think you need to, Ash, just tell him you haven't been able to recreate the experiment yet." Mican chuckled. "That's job security for at least five years, but I do think we need to call Shay." He tapped her number into his phone, when she answered, he put her on speak phone. "Hello, Serious Trainee McKnight."

Her voice almost crackled it was so high. "How'd you know that? Are you watching me?"

"Not like you think, but Ash and I are here together in the park. He called me earlier today and told me he saw a dark shadow creeping up on you in the gym."

Ashton pulled Mican's arm toward his mouth. "Hi Shay, I was working in the lab trying to make a portal out of a mirror and I saw your image."

Her voice leapt. "So, you were successful?"

"Not exactly."

Mican interrupted. "He stepped out into the hall

to call me. We prayed for you and when he felt peace, he went back in, his coworkers told him you had hurled some big dude over your shoulder."

Ashton continued. "When your image cleared from the mirror, Mican's appeared. I had to step out and pray for him too."

"Was he in danger?"

Ashton chuckled. "Only in danger of not getting the funding he was after. When I prayed for him a man and a dark cloud left the room."

"I don't understand, Ash, why don't you think you were successful?"

Ashton's hands flopped to his side. "I had no control of it."

"So how did you see Jager call me a serious trainee?" her voice got deep, "and you didn't see the rest of it, did you?"

"Yes, we did, sis, Ash and I met in the park to talk things over and a puddle of water next us turned into the same type of visual gateway as his mirror. We saw the guy running at you."

Ashton leaned to the phone. "I yelled to warn you

and Mican prayed that no weapon formed against you would prosper and we hadn't even seen the knife yet, so we know that was a word from Abba."

Mican added, "You were super, sis, I was amazed!"

Shayla stopped him. "Hmm, that makes sense, I did hear someone yell, 'look out,' but both times when I flipped that guy, he felt like a feather, so that had to be Abba too. Why do you think this is happening? Seeing the images and me getting attacked, I mean."

Mican rubbed his chin. "I don't know, Shay, unless the temperature is being turned up?"

"I don't get it, what'd ya' mean?"

Ashton looked at his brother. "I think he means, that since you've been tapped for Quantico, there's a higher degree of spiritual warfare coming against you. You must be there for a very important reason."

Mican nodded. "That's exactly what I mean, Ash."

Shayla paused for a moment. "That must be why I keep sending Jager away. He's a really nice guy and cute, but I don't think I need to get involved with anyone. Ash, why do you think you saw Mican?"

They stared at each other for a moment, then Mican added. "Maybe the temperature is being turned up on all of us. I got the funding I was seeking for the Copper Scroll project and when I told Dr. Dodds, he decided to send someone else because I didn't want to leave Maddy right now. You know, sis, I think Jesus is coming again soon and we all have a lot of work to do to prepare the way."

"I agree Mican, what about you, Ash?"

Mican noticed his brother's face. "Ash what's wrong? Don't you agree?"

"I do agree that Jesus is coming back soon, I feel it in my spirit. I'm just wondering if I'm wasting my time trying to pretend that I'm opening portals when we all know it's Abba doing it."

Shayla's voice snapped him to attention. "Ashton McKnight, you know that Abba would speak to you if you were wasting your time and I think Max and dad would realize it too. They seem to be at peace with where you are and even helped to direct you that way. Besides," there was a slight pause and her voice changed. "If you go to the zoo every morning, how do you get to your lab?"

Ashton burst out laughing. "Great Segway, Shay and to answer your question, I go out the back of the butterfly building, get in a golf cart with a herpetologist, entomologist and primatologist, drive to the back of the lot, to a metal door in the wall, one of us swipes a key card and we all go downstairs into an underground tunnel, walk about a quarter mile and emerge in the lab. Any more questions?" Laughter returned from him and Mican.

"I simply wanted to know, you two, stop laughing at me." She turned her question to her oldest brother. "Mican where do you work?"

"At the University, Shay. I walk into the Archeology Building, turn right and go into my office."

"Is that all, no secret panels or anything?"

"Nope! That's it, a plain ol' office."

"Well that's boring." She paused then laughed. "Only joking! Thanks for calling and for watching my back, literally. I've got to run, I have a class at Hogan's Alley and I'm running late."

They could hear the smile in her voice. Mican leaned to the phone. "We love you, Shay-Belle, may the Lord cover you with his feathers."[xxiv]

A spontaneous giggle followed. "And many feathers to you two, my sweet brothers."

Ashton pulled Mican's sleeve to be closer to the phone. "And may Abba deliver you from the snare of the fowler and the arrow that flies by day."[xxv]

Mican pulled his arm back to his face. "And you shall not be afraid of the terror by night."[xxvi]

Shayla jumped in. "And with long life he satisfies us and shows us his salvation."[xxvii]

Her brothers laughed, then Ashton added. "Ninety-one is a great Psalm, probably my favorite."

Her oldest brother's tone softened. "We love you, Shay-Belle."

"Thanks, Mican. I love you both so much, bye."

Mican closed his phone.

Ashton took a step back and jerked his hands up from his sides. "Do you realize we just wasted a perfectly good opportunity to tease our sister about Jager?"

Mican chuckled. "Let's head home. Do you need a lift to the zoo parking lot to get your car?"

"Yes, if you don't mind, it's a long way around to the lot and I can't go back through the store it's locked and I told the other *ologists* to go ahead without me."

Mican clapped his hand on his brother's back. "Do ya' want to go talk to our folks?"

Chapter 19

Hogan's Alley

Following the phone call with her brothers, Shayla headed to her next class at Hogan's Alley.[xxviii] She waved at Jager and shouted, "Because of the attack and a call from my brothers, I'm running late, can you give he a lift?"

"Sure! Hop in."

She jumped into his jeep and he stepped on the pedal. She arrived right on time, but Jager started to walk her to the place where her class gathered. "That's okay, I'm fine. Thanks, for the lift."

"I'll walk the rest of the way with you, if you're late, I can vouch for your excuse, plus, I guess this is as close as I'll get to a date with you," he laughed.

The Instructor yelled, "No visitors! Clear the field."

Jager saluted the trainer and turned to Shayla. "Guess you don't need me after all, bye, McKnight," he chuckled, "thanks for the date."

After the Instructor announced the assignments, Shayla darted to her designated building. She bent her knees, tucked in tight and crept inside. Just before the door closed, she saw a tall shadow, then darkness engulfed her, she paused to allow time for her eyes to adjust. She pulled her flashlight from her lower leg pocket, but felt a check in her spirit, *no light, trust me.* She felt a nudge in her spirit to move to her left, she obeyed and at that moment something whizzed past her head and clanked against the metal wall behind her. *I shall not be afraid of the arrow that flies by day, thank you, Abba.* She continued forward, *I must have about ten more feet to go before I'm halfway through the building.* At that point she felt a nudge to freeze and lean further to her left, when she leaned, she knocked against something and dropped to the floor as a deluge of feathers fell from above. She heard movement to her right, but only a crack of light filtered through the plumage.

One voice whispered, "Where'd she go?"

The second, "You must have let her slip past you, you idiot."

The first guy spoke again. "I did not, you must 'ave."

A harsh brutish voice scolded him. "Shut up and get to the back and guard the target. I'll go outside and around to the back door so she can't get out with the flag."

The first man laughed. "She can't get it?"

"How do you know?"

He turned his back to the second man and pointed to his rump with his flashlight. "Cause, I have it in my back pocket."

The second man laughed. "Well, let's capture her anyway, maybe the instructor will let us torture her." They both chuckled.

The door cracked open and Shayla saw through

the feathers that the man left inside was much larger than herself. *Abba, what am I to do?* She waited and heard the backdoor open. The man to her right moved a few steps toward his compatriot, he scanned his light to the left and right as he walked. When he was several feet away, Shayla lunged from beneath the pile of feathers and grabbed the dude's back pocket, ripping it as she stole the flag.

Shocked, he jerked around, Shayla was almost at the exit.

Her opponent dashed toward her like a football player and slammed his body against the door before she could escape.

She screamed, "Abba!"

The man grabbed her and feathers whooshed from her hair and fluttered into his face. His head reared back as a sneeze welled up in his nose. He jerked his hands up and when he sneezed his head flew forward and slammed against the steel door. He dropped to the floor like a sack of rocks.

Shayla pulled his legs away from the door and forced it open. As his partner entered the area, she held the flag high over her head, whooped, dashed outside and ran to the safety zone at the feet of the instructor.

"Good work, McKnight!" The instructor placed a mark by her name on his list. "How did you figure out how to evade those two big guys?"

"Again, sir, Hide and Seek and I have two older brothers, Sir!"

He chuckled. "You may make a good agent yet."

"Thank you, sir!" She bent and placed her hands on her knees and whispered, "Thank you, Abba."

Chapter 20

That Night

Tired from the day's schedule, Shayla nestled into her bed with her nightstand lamp on to study her next assignment in Arabic, but she dozed and her head drooped forward, causing her to awake to darkness. The sense of a presence in her room overtook her. "Marcy, are you here?" No response came. "Who's here?"

A disguised voice spoke into one ear. "You got my friend arrested."

She pulled her head away from the voice. "I didn't do anything but defend myself."

From the other side she heard, "You embarrassed him in the gym."

"That's not my fault. He was taking the exercise

way too serious when he came at me, my instincts kicked in and I threw him."

"You could have let him take you down."

Infuriated, she belted out, "I will never fake any exercise for the sake of some man's ego." Springing to her feet, she leapt toward the foot of the bed and brushed past a net as she lurched forward, turned and shouted, "Abba will deliver me from the snare of the fowler,[xxix] his word says it and it's true. I am his child and I'm here at his command. You have no authority over me."

Shayla felt a thud as the two brutes lunged for her, she sprang into the air, balled her fists tight, and bent her arms as she fell to her knees, her elbows landing a blow on the back of each thug's head. *Luckily the mattress pad Max packed for me eased the impact to my knees as I landed those blows.*

At that moment, the light switch flipped on, a shadow in the corner vanished.

Marcy's voice erupted. "See I told you I saw two men sneaking down here."

Two security personnel dashed toward the tangle

of flesh. Jager pulled Shayla off the bed. "You again, McKnight? How many men did you wound this time?" he chuckled.

"Very funny, Jager." She rubbed her elbows. "These two were part of the exercise I won today at Hogan's Alley. They're friends of the guy you arrested earlier for attacking me."

He wagged his head. "If you keep this up, McKnight, we won't have any big guys left to graduate." He used his walkie to call for back up.

Within seconds, others arrived and arrested the two men who lay dazed on Shayla's bed. Jager picked up the two nets and tossed them to one of the Security Guards. "Take these and log them into evidence, these guys will see some prison time for trespassing, attempted assault and attempted kidnapping, at the very least. We may find some other charges if we put our minds to it."

Everyone cleared the room except Marcy, Shayla and Jager.

Marcy came over and patted her shoulder. "Girl, are you okay?"

"Yeah, thanks Marcy, I'll be fine, I just need to call one of my brothers and do some processing to calm down."

Jager stared at the floor. "McKnight, may I speak with you in the hall."

She nodded and they walked out, the Security Guard closed the door behind him. "Shayla, do you know why this is happening to you? And how you are subduing these big guys?"

"I can't talk to you, Jager, I need to talk to my brothers."

"It's late Shayla do you really want to call and wake them up with news that you've been attacked again?"

She hung her head. "No, I guess you're right."

Jager folded his arms. "Why can't you talk to me? I'm a nice guy."

With her head shaking side-to-side, she asked, "What're you even doing on duty? Every time I turn around you're there." She smiled. "Are you stalking me?"

His head dropped forward and his arms fell to his

sides. "No McKnight, *I'm* not stalking you, I'm just following orders."

She shook her head. "I need to talk to someone who knows things. Would you believe that today on the phone, my brother Mican spoke over me that I'd be covered with feathers, and that's how I hid from those goons in the Hogan exercise. And my brother Ashton prayed I'd not be afraid of the arrow that flies by day, and one of them shot an arrow at me. And he prayed that I'd be protected from the fowler's snare, and those two baboons that just got hauled out of here had nets."

Jager folded his arms. "Yeah, Psalm ninety-one, right?"

Shayla's mouth sank open. "You know Psalm ninety-one?"

He plopped his hands at his waist. "Yes, Shayla, I do, I know lots of things."

"Well, my brother, Ashton knew I was in danger this morning and called our brother Mican and he prayed that Abba would launch his warring angels to protect me."

Folding his arms again, he replied, "So, I could pray that for you too."

Her lips tightened. "But," she spread her hands slightly to the side and her head bobbed toward him. "it's how they knew to pray for me when I was in danger."

Jager closed his eyes, when he opened them again, he said, "Abba, showed Ashton a picture in the mirror, I don't exactly understand how that worked, but … you get the picture."

Shayla's mouth flew open. "You know Abba?"

Chapter 21

Big Shock

"Sure, I take my orders from him. Why do you think I keep showing up when you're in trouble? By the way, you can call me Gabriel, I'm Gabriel Jager and jager is German for *hunter*."[xxx]

She chuckled. "So, what are you hunting, Gabriel, a date?"

He placed his hands on his hips and leveled his gaze at her. "No Shayla, I'm not hunting a date, I'm hunting the demon that's stalking you!"

Without any control, her shoulders jerked back and her arms stiffened at her sides. "What do you mean, a demon is stalking me?"

"I mean exactly what I said, Shayla," his right index finger pointed at her, "you're being stalked by a demonic presence. Haven't you wondered how three thugs like those guys could have gotten into Quantico? I checked the first man's record after the event this morning and by all accounts, he was an excellent recruit, but something happened to him and probably to his two friends also. I suspect that the demon got a foothold with them and was driving their actions, now their careers are ruined because of some weakness the demon was able to exploit."

"So why you, Jager?"

"Because I'm an archangel sent to protect you."

Touching his arm, she blinked. "An angel? But you feel real."

"Angels can take on a corporeal body,"[xxxi] he spread his hands and glanced down, "as you see here, and I'm usually assigned to deliver a message to a particular person[xxxii] or to protect certain people and to hunt and capture entities who attempt to interfere with Abba's plans. Have you noticed a dark figure lurking near you?"

"Yes, I saw it earlier today when that guy rushed at me and again at the Hogan's Alley exercise, but I thought that one was a shadow of one of my opponents and I saw it again in my room tonight when you first opened the door, but it vanished, I thought I imagined it, but my brother said he saw a shadowy figure in the first picture he saw of me earlier today."

"Did you see it at the Trailing Exercise?"

She thought for a minute. "I felt a struggle on top of the box I was hiding under, then when I was able to lift it, I saw two streaks, one light and one dark heading away from me."

"That was me and the demonic spirit, I almost captured him then, but in the struggle, he eluded me because I lagged behind to be sure you were all right. Sometimes these encounters can make the victim dizzy and disoriented."

"You're right, I was dizzy for a moment," her hands flew wide to the side, "but why is it stalking *me*?"

"Shayla, you have a mighty calling on your life, as is evidenced by the fact that at age seventeen, Abba chose you to rescue kids who were being trafficked.[xxxiii] He also gave you the ability to do that and not to carry any residual effects of the horrible things you saw."

"You know, you're right! I never thought of it before, but I've never had a single nightmare or even a bad dream about what I saw or heard. That's amazing! Thank you, Abba!"

"You're right to be thankful, Shayla, but even before people are born, Abba knows them. He places a wellspring of potential in each person, it's up to them and their parents to measure out the potential at each stage as they grow. Your parents and you have done well in this assignment, your Mom and Dad started you on your journey, she did well on her own after the death of your father, then she and your stepdad continued to guide you, and you've continued very strongly as an adult, you Shayla Marie McKnight are a true treasure. If I were allowed to marry, you would be my choice, but angels are not allowed to marry, though some of the Watchers' Class did take human young women as wives, but it didn't work out well for them or their offspring."[xxxiv]

Leaning forward her eyes narrowed. "Why didn't it work out well for them?"

"The Watcher angels that defied Abba's rules and took human women for wives were cast into Tartarus.[xxxv] Their children became known as men of renown,[xxxvi] they were giants, also known as the Nephilim and the souls of these giants, after the death of their earthly bodies, roam this world as demonic spirits. Those beings are not fully human, so their spirits can't go to heaven, and they're from the rebellious angels who fell, so neither can their spirits return to heaven as an angelic being; therefore, they're doomed to roam the earth, hungering and thirsting for what they cannot have as spirit or as flesh."

Shayla's forehead wrinkled. "That's sad."

Jager lamented. "Yes, it is, but rebellion, or sin of any kind, has its price. For a human, the wage of sin is death,[xxxvii] for an angel, it's very different, but still very costly."

"Thanks, for giving me that understanding, Jager."

"You're welcome Shayla, you're one of the purest souls I've ever encountered and you are in my charge. I will stay as close to you as is needed to protect you until your husband is revealed. He is a mighty warrior and when he arrives, I will not be needed to cover you, but for now, you may call on me at any time, day or night, and I shall be there. Goodnight, Shayla!" and he vanished.

Glancing around, her arms sprang up. "Husband? Jager," she shouted, "you said 'my husband is a mighty warrior.' Who is he?"

Chapter 22

At Their Parents' Home

When Mom opened the door, she greeted her sons with a large smile. "Come in, boys, after you phoned, I called the girls and Max, to invite them over for dinner."

Mican laughed. "Yeah, after we got your permission to come over, we had enough sense to call our wives and tell them our plan to stop by, they informed us that you had already invited us all for dinner."

They served their plates from the kitchen and took their usual seats in the dining room. Mom's eyes glanced from face-to-face, then paused at the empty chair. Shayla's place remained conspicuously vacant.

Tom Phillips took his cue. "Dear Heavenly Father, thank you that most of our family have been able to join us this evening. Continue to watch over our daughter and bless this food, in Jesus' name, amen."

Mican leaned his elbows on the table. "Mom, we have something to tell you about Shayla."

Candice rose in her chair. "Is she okay?"

"Yes, ma'am, take it easy, but I wanted the family to know that Ash and I think the spiritual heat has been turned up. Do you remember when Shay went to the Police Academy and you felt a heaviness in the air?"

"I remember."

Tom nodded. "I remember too. We did some serious praying for her and all of you kids."

Ashton smiled. "We remember Philly and we appreciate it, that's why we want you to know what we found out today."

Mom shook her head. "Found out?"

"Well, what we saw today." Ashton leaned back. "Let me start over." He looked at Max and Philly.

"You remember the secret program I got into with the FBI?"

Everyone nodded.

"Well today, I was trying to open a travel portal, but I accessed a visual gateway, like a window, instead. At least I thought it was me, but it didn't take long to figure out it was Abba doing it. Anyway, he showed me Shayla in a gym with a dark shadow creeping up on her. I went out into the hall and called Mican." He smiled at his brother. "Mican went into high gear praying for her and actually asked Abba to *launch* warring angels to her, it was awesome." He turned back to his mother. "Anyway, I guess she was in a self-defense class because she was in her exercise sweats and she took care of this really big guy, *but* and this is the important thing, I'm not sure she would have been successful without Mican's prayer. Later, after work, Mican and I got together to discuss this and Abba activated a puddle near our feet as a visual portal, we saw the same guy racing toward Shayla. Mican instantly prayed that no weapon formed against her would prosper and Shayla grabbed the guy, rolled over onto her back and sent the guy flying! A guard with base security witnessed the whole thing and arrested the dude."

Mom slapped her hands together in front of her. "That's wonderful."

Ashton lowered his head and continued. "But mom, he had a knife."

Candice gasped. "He had what? But you said she's safe, right?"

"Yes ma'am, but we believe the spiritual heat is being turned up on her and maybe on all of us as well. We all need to *up* our prayers. Shayla must be at Quantico for some really big reason because the enemy has already started to attack her."

Tom jumped in. "In Jesus name, the powers of darkness will not prevail over Shayla or any member of this family, including our daughters-in-law and Max. Father, please cover each of us with the blood of Jesus, amen!"

Candice turned to her husband and patted his hand. "Thank you, Tom, you've always been such a blessing and encouragement to me, and thank you for loving my kids like they were your very own."

Tom smiled. "They are my own, sweetie, I love you and all of them."

Mican turned to his wife. "Maddy, I got the funding today for the scroll project, but Dodds wanted me to leave immediately. I tried to negotiate with him to postpone my trip until after the first of the year, but he refused."

Wide eyes, teared up. "You have to leave now, before the baby's born?"

He put his arm around Madelaine. "No, honey, he's going to send Marks in my place."

Candice's mouth sagged open. "But, Mican, that's not fair, that's your project."

Ashton patted Mican on the shoulder. "We prayed and put it in Abba's hands, we'll see what he does. Mican will either be able to go after the new year or something better will come up for him."

Mom passed the dinner, to a rather quiet group, but everyone seemed pleased with the meal.

Chapter 23

Captive Exercise

"Listen up, trainees, today we're going to practice escaping from an armed assailant. Team up with another person and one of you will be the captive and the other will be the captor. Here's the written assignment, familiarize yourselves with it and I'll meet you in the theater in twenty minutes."

Shayla turned to a fellow student. "Blake, do you want to team up with me?"

"Yeah, Shay, thanks, I think you'll make me look good."

She folded her arms. "How do you mean, Blake?"

"Isn't it obvious? I'll be the captor and there's no way you'll ever get away from me." He put his hands on his hips and laughed.

"I don't think so, Blake, if you want to look really good, you be the captive and get away from me."

He folded his arms and tipped his head back. "Yeah, right!"

"Okay, Blake, have it your way, but I tried to warn you."

They read the assignment and got the necessary items for their event, Blake chose a knife as his weapon. Twenty minutes later, the instructor met everyone in the designated area. "Okay, trainees, listen up. Whoever is the captor, will have one opportunity to hold your hostage for five minutes. If the captive cannot escape, the trainee playing the role of captor gets the point. If the captive escapes in the allotted time, that trainee gets the point. Understood?"

The students all shouted, "Yes, sir!"

"Okay, let the mayhem begin. McKnight, who's your partner?"

"Blake is, sir."

"Which of you will be the captor?"

Blake puffed out his chest. "I will, sir."

The instructor said, "That's a shocker! Okay, McKnight, you'll be the captive. We will take it from the point where you've been subdued and are in zip-ties. Set the scene!"

Blake pulled a wooden chair into the center of a circle drawn on the floor. He turned Shayla with her back to him and started to apply the zip-ties.

Shayla whispered over her shoulder, "If you zip me in back, you can't tie me to the chair, my hands will be in the way."

He roughly turned her around, crossed her wrists and applied the zip in the front and growled, "Sit down."

She sat in the chair and he wrapped a rope around her shoulders and arms above the elbows, tying it in the back.

Blake nodded to the instructor.

"McKnight, you have five minutes to escape, starting," he lifted the stopwatch and clicked it, "now!"

Shayla let out the large breath she'd been

holding. This loosened the rope enough that she could shimmy it up her body to her shoulders. She lifted her zipped wrists pushing the rope up higher, moved the square fasteners the tie to the center between her wrists, leaned forward, lifting the two back chair legs off the floor. She straightened as much as the situation would allow, yelled as she brought her wrist down in front of her, twisting them at the bottom of the maneuver, pushing her hands out to the sides, breaking the zip-tie. Holding on to the arms of the chair, she lifted it with her back and propelled herself backwards, the legs pointing at Blake.

In shock, Blake lifted the knife and shifted himself to the side.

Shayla saw the movement out of the corner of her eye and growled as she swung the chair wildly toward him, using her now free hands to help guide her retaliation.

The instructor caught the chair a split-second before it would have knocked Blake off his feet or out of the circle. "Okay, McKnight, let's say you've disabled your captor, what then?"

She placed the chair on the floor and wiggled the ropes up to her neck and lifted them off with her hands, but noticed her bleeding wrists.

The instructor clapped. "Good work, McKnight, where'd you learn to fight like that?"

"I'm a former police officer, sir! And I have two older brothers, sir!"

The instructor chuckled, then gave an order. "Now go to the infirmary."

"Thank you, sir, but if you don't mind, I'd like to stay and see the rest of the scenarios."

He nodded, "But then get those cuts tended too."

"Yes, sir." She took a seat in the gallery for the rest of the exercise.

Chapter 24

Another Window

Ashton worked feverishly, though felt he struggled in vain, until one day, three weeks after his first encounter with the visual portal, his contraption whirred again, a cloud spun, then dissolved as a window opened and there, Mican stood before a group of people, he was dressed in a suit and was speaking, but no audio accompanied the scene. *This looks familiar! Where've I seen this picture before?* A flash of remembrance crossed his mind. *This is what Abba showed us when we were young. Abba called Mican up first and his life began to flash on a screen behind Abba's throne. This is that!*[xxxviii] *But Abba is this now? Is it at this moment? The picture you showed me of Shayla was in real* *time. Is this in real time too?*

Co-workers gathered around his workstation.

One of them shouted, "Sadie, get the professor, I'll get the camera."

Seconds later the program director raced to Ashton's side, workers gave way to allow him a good view at Ashton's right, the video camera rolled to Ashton's left.

With lightning fast mental speed, Ashton prayed an internal monologue. *Father, bless and guide Mican. I'm not sure what you want for him in this situation, but I ask that your will be done. Cover him with your protection, power and glory, in Jesus' name, amen.*

The image clouded and spun to a frosted screen, then returned to a regular mirror.

Dr. Clarence, clapped his hand on Ashton's back. "Well done, my boy, let's see the video, then you can take us through your process again."

Kyle turned the camera to replay and held it before the group, but all that was on the screen was static.

Irritation in Dr. Clarence's voice confronted Kyle. "You must be doing something wrong," the camera drooped in his hands. "Twice, you've failed to film this momentous occurrence. I want Richard to man the camera from now on, give it to him."

Kyle turned to his coworker and handed over the device.

The program director turned his attention back to Ashton.

Sweat began to bead on the back of Ashton's neck. *What do I do Abba? I know it was you. Give me words and touch Kyle's wounded spirit.*

"Show us your steps Ashton, one-by-one walk us through what you did."

Ashton reached up, turned knobs and wiggled wires, but to no avail.

A stern voice demanded. "What's wrong, young man? Are you deliberately withholding your work? This is supposed to be a collaborative effort."

Ashton faced the professor. "No, sir! I'm not withholding anything. This is just unstable. I can't reproduce the work at will." A thought struck his mind. "Perhaps it's a string or an event that comes into proximity with the device, then it activates, but the strings are in constant motion. Maybe if we could find a way to track the events, we could program the device to locate them or we could follow them in a vehicle and, sir, with all due respect, I don't think it was Kyle's fault or a faulty camera. Perhaps the camera needs to be recalibrated to scan the static for a picture."

The professor folded his left arm across his midsection, propping his right elbow on his left hand and stroked his chin with his right index finger. "You may have a point McKnight. Choose a team to work with you on the theory of a moving event and how to locate it."

Ashton smiled. "Yes, sir, I will, immediately."

"Richard, you work to see if the camera can be recalibrated to reveal the picture," The director turned and walked away.

Kyle approached. "Thanks for speaking up for me. I don't think the professor likes me because I'm a Christian. He told me that we should stick to science, not old wives' tales. I appreciate you going out a limb for me like that."

"Kyle who else here is a Christian, do you know?"

"Janet and I have talked some, so I know she is and I think Marcus is too."

"Great," Ashton held up his hand, "Janet, would you and Marcus join me and Kyle at my station."

The two approached.

Ashton smiled at them. "Would you two, like to join Kyle and me on researching the possibility of a mobile event causing the instability of my device?"

With enthusiasm, Janet nodded. "I would love too, when you said that earlier to the professor, my spirit jumped inside me."

Marcus stared at her.

She drew her shoulders back. "What, Marcus?"

He lowered his voice. "I thought I was being silly, but my insides jumped too."

Ashton received a nudge in his spirt. *One more!* He walked to the center of the room. "Okay, listen up, I'm looking for special people to join my team."

He smiled. "How many of you have time traveled?"

Several people burst out laughing, Ashton scanned the room, but one person stared at the floor. "Zane, would you like to join us?"

His face lifted. "Really? Sure thing."

Ashton waited in the center of the workspace until Zane joined him and they strolled toward Ashton's station, he whispered, "So, Zane, where did Abba, send you when you time traveled?"

His head jerked to the side and wild eyes stared at Ashton. "Let's just say, I wasn't in Kansas anymore,"[xxxix] and he smiled.

Ashton assumed Zane was trying to determine if he was joking. "We'll talk later, my fellow Kansan," and he smiled back at Zane.

Chapter 25

Telling the Tale

Ashton waited until after work to call his brother. "Hey dude, are you wearing your gray tweed jacket, gray pants, white shirt and a sweet silver tie?"

"How'd you know that, Ash?"

"Abba let me see a picture of you today. By the way, I prayed for you. How'd your meeting work out?"

Excitement bubbled on the other end of the phone. "Ash, I got the largest endowment that my department's ever gotten. This will firm up our scroll project for three full years."

"Congrats, dude, I didn't know what to pray, so I prayed that Abba's will be done and I guess it was, oh, and another thing, do you remember the picture that Abba showed you behind his throne, of when you were grown?"

"Yeah, why?"

"That was it, dude, I mean today, in that room with those people, that was the scene he showed you."

"Really?"

"Yeah, man, you probably couldn't tell because you were standing in it, but it was the same scene."

A pause broke the excitement until, Mican shouted. "Ash, Abba just showed it to me again, in my mind, you're right, this was it." Another pause and his voice took on an ominous tone. "So, does that mean my career is over?" Suddenly laughter broke out.

"What's up, Mican?"

Another momentary pause, "I was driving and I had to pull over. Abba was flashing picture after picture in my mind. I was getting so excited, I was afraid I'd wreck, so I had to stop."

"That's great, are you calm enough to talk now?"

"Yeah, yeah, you're funny."

"Good, after I saw you and the picture faded, Dr. Clarence demanded that I recreate the event. Of course, you know I couldn't and he accused me of withholding my research."

"What'd you do?"

"Abba helped me keep my cool and gave me a *string theory* possibility to present. That gave the director something to think about and told me to form a team to research my idea. It was then that I found three Christians working in the lab. Abba told me there was one more, so do you remember when Shayla gave the suggestion of asking who'd time traveled before? Well, it worked. I stepped to the center of the room and asked that, most people laughed, but I saw a guy in the back stare at the floor, so I called him to join my team. As we walked back to my station, I asked him where he'd traveled to, he wasn't sure if I was serious or not, so he used the *Wizard of Oz* line that he wasn't in Kansas anymore. Isn't that great?"

"That is great, Ash, but be sure to tell Shayla and give our little sis her props."

"I plan to, she's my next call. Talk to you later, bro."

Ashton ended his call with Mican and used voice assist to dial Shayla. "Hi sis, have you got a minute?"

A serious tone greeted him. "Sure, Ash, is everything okay?"

"Yeah, I just have something great to tell you?"

Her voice hit a high pitch. "Has Madelaine had the baby?"

"Geez Louise, take it down a notch, Auntie Shay. No, it's not that, though she's due to pop any day now."

Her normal voice returned. "Okay, sorry, so what's up?"

"Do you remember your suggestion to ask who'd been time traveling? I used it today. I had already unearthed three Christians in the lab and your idea produced a fourth."

"Great, Ash, I'm glad to hear it. Did you find out where Abba took him?"

"Not yet, but I'll keep you informed. So how are things at the Big Q?"

"Wow, Quantico is tough, but I'm loving every minute of it. Right now, I have bandages around my wrists."

Ashton laughed. "So, you won the captive-captor exercise, right?"

"Yeah, how'd you know?"

"People who escape the zip-ties, always end up with bandages."

"You're right!" she laughed, "I can hardly believe that graduation is right around the corner."

His head tipped back and he laughed. "You think you're excited, Mom's already started a countdown calendar."

Shayla joined his laughter. "Me too, I'll be home in twenty-one days! Time's flown since the first week of August."

"The family can't wait to hear all about your new assignment, sis." A beep, Ashton pulled the phone away to look at the screen. "I've got to run, Mican is calling me back, love ya, sis!"

Chapter 26

You Won't Believe It

Ashton answered to hear the feverish voice of his brother. "Ash, I just got a call from Dr. Dodds, I can't believe it, John Marks was supposed to be in Jordan, but the Copper Scroll Project Director called and asked the professor where *I* was and why *I* hadn't shown up."

"Hadn't he called to tell him of the personnel change?"

"Dodds thought he'd called, but the project director told him he never got the message. The director had continued to wait, because he said he knew *I* was reliable and figured there was a problem. Well, the prof called Marks to see what had happened. John hadn't wanted to tell the professor that his passport had been flagged, he wanted to try to get it straightened out without telling the professor, but the Copper Scroll Project manager had asked Dodds why *I* wasn't coming. Dodds told him I wanted to wait because of our baby being due, so he had assigned someone else. The manager blew a fuse and insisted that he change the position back to me and that I be sent over after the first of the year. When Dodds asked why the change of time, the director told him they were moving to a different office location within the museum and he wouldn't need me to help move, so I could come after the first of the year. Isn't that great? Abba worked it out, bro, just like you prayed he would."

"Woohoo!"

Mican laughed. "You're sounding more like Bailey every day."

Ashton laughed. "Yeah, I'm afraid she's rubbing off on me, she hooked me fifteen years ago by calling me a *boat,* when I found out it was short for dreamboat, I was sunk," he laughed, "and thanks for sharing your marvelous news, dude. Congrats!"

A beep on Mican's end. "Ooops, gotta go, Maddy's calling me."

Chapter 27

At the Hospital

The maternity waiting room was awash with people. Candice paced, Tom and Max played cards, Ashton and Bailey giggled in a cozy corner, until Mican rushed in. "It's a girl!"

Everyone raced to greet him.

"Maddy is fine and Candice Elaine is fine!"

His mom clenched her hands to her chest. "Oh honey, that's so sweet. Thank you for including my name in hers."

"Not a problem, Mom and we included Madelaine's late mom's name too, Elaine. We couldn't figure out how to combine Maddy's name and mine to make a decent girl's name so we took the two grandmothers' names and we're going to call her

Candy-E. The only other closest alternatives were Candee, Candel, or Candelaine." He laughed. "The first sounded too much in favor of you, Mom, and the second sounded like –you got it—a candle and the third sounded too much like a kids' board game."

Everyone laughed.

Mom leaned in to kiss him on his cheek. "Candy-E sounds perfect, when can we see Maddy and the baby?"

"It'll be a few minutes. Can someone call Shay? I need to get back in the room."

From the back of the group, they heard Bailey's voice. "It's a girl, they're going to call her Candy-E for the grandmothers, Candice and Elaine."

Mican laughed. "I guess Shay's covered."

Chapter 28

Reviewing the Schedule

Shayla strolled toward the gun range. *I can't believe how busy I've been, but also how fast time's flown. Self-defense classes have been great since Godzilla got arrested, but I'm sorry that ruined his whole career. We're down to the last two weeks. I can't believe it, today's our final review in marksmanship.*

"McKnight, you're up next, the target is at sixty yards. You're required to have one hundred and ten hours of training here at Quantico, this is your final assessment, you have five rounds left to complete your five thousand rounds fired, but I hear you've been putting in a little extra practice. Let's see how you do."

Lying down for the first three shots, Shayla aimed and fired. She reset herself and fired again. Aiming, she let loose her third shot.

"Now standing, McKnight."

Shayla got to her knees and stood without pushing. She steadied her-self and fired. Reset, took a deep breath, let the breath out and fired.

"Stand clear, McKnight." The instructor picked up his field glasses and looked down range. "Five out of five, dead center. Where'd you learn to shoot like that, McKnight?"

"I grew up in Tennessee, sir, I was formerly in law enforcement and I have two …"

The instructor finished her sentence. "Yeah, yeah, and you have two older brothers, you're dismissed McKnight!"

Retrieving her folder from her book bag, *let me see, the rest of my day's schedule consists of assessments in finger printing, Hostage Negotiation at the Bank, voice recognition, hmmm, I think my ear is getting pretty good in voice recognition and one more escape exercise.*

Shayla entered the Dogwood Inn Restaurant, for her next class in fingerprint assessment.

The instructor approached. "McKnight, you're wanted in the Director's office immediately after class."

Oh no, what have I done now. "Yes, sir!"

As instructed, immediately following fingerprint assessment, Shayla entered the Admin building. "Hi Timmens, how's everything?"

"Great Shayla, how are you doing?"

"Classes are going well, but I've been ordered to see the director. Any idea what that's about?"

"Not a clue, but I'll let his secretary know you're on your way."

"Thanks, Timmens."

Upstairs, the secretary was waiting, "Hello Trainee McKnight. The Director is ready for you, go right in."

She tapped on the glass and opened the door. "You wanted to see me, sir?"

"Yes, McKnight, please be seated."

Shayla seated herself in a chair, sitting erect, feet together and hands in her lap.

The director sat behind his desk, across from her. "It has come to my attention, Trainee McKnight that someone has been requesting your grades. Now normally that would not be allowed, but you, young woman have some powerful people checking on you. Based on preliminary scores, they have asked me to pass on their desires that, following your graduation, you attend the U.S. Marshals Academy before receiving your final assignment. I would seriously consider accepting their invitation, if I were you. You will receive the formal, written request just prior to graduation, but I wanted you to know how special this invitation is. Think it over trainee. You're dismissed."

She stood. "Yes, Sir, thank you, Sir," and turned toward the door.

Downstairs, when she reached the desk, with a big smile, Timmens laughed and asked, "In trouble again?"

Shayla smiled, but shook her head *no*, then her brows knit tight. "Just another invitation, this one is to attend the U.S. Marshals Academy."

Timmens' eyebrows shot up. "What? Girl, you've got someone in your corner."

Shayla opened the door, turned, smiled and said, "I know, right?"

Her last op exercise for the day was the Captive-Captor Assessment. She arrived at Hogan's Alley in time to hear the instructor say, "Blake, you want a chance to redeem your self-esteem by being partnered with McKnight again?"

He jerked to attention. "Yes, Sir!"

"Okay, here's your scenario," he handed them each a piece of paper, "and McKnight," the instructor chuckled, "try not to hurt Blake."

Shayla smiled. "Yes, Sir, I'll do my best not to, Sir."

Blake's eyes flashed at her with fury.

Uh oh, Abba, I need your help.

The instructor barked. "Set the scene, we'll begin with the hostage bound and the captor outside the room standing guard."

Shayla stuck her hands out in front.

Blake growled. "No way, hostage, turn around." He bound her hands tightly behind her back, then grabbed a second set of ties. "Stand still, but cross your ankles."

Shayla followed his orders.

When he finished he whispered in her ear, "Try to get out of that!"

Shayla swayed to get her balance.

The instructor shouted. "You have five minutes McKnight. Go!"

Shayla closed her eyes. *Abba, if it's your desire for me to escape, you have to show me how, in Jesus' name.* A tune rushed into her mind, with the words of a song, filling her ears. *In the corners of my mind, I just can't seem to find a reason to believe that I can break free.*[xl] With a rush of joy, a smile filled her face, she began to bounce around to music only she could hear, up onto her tiptoes then down, causing her knees to swish back and forth, shifting her shoulders, she began to sing. "Take the shackles off my feet so I can dance,"[xli] hopping around, the ties on her feet began to loosen.[xlii]

Blake, outside guarding the door, rushed in and dove for her feet, just as one side of the ties broke free and Shayla's kick caught him under the chin.

Raising her voice, she sang and danced, "I just want to praise you, I just want to praise you."[xliii]

Stretched out on the floor, Blake's mouth flew open. "No way!"

She bumped against a rough post, still wiggling her shoulders, she began to scrape the zip ties against the ragged wood, then with one good yank, they snapped, as she threw her hands in the air, she belted out the next verse. "You broke the chains now I can lift my hands. And I'm gonna praise you. I'm gonna praise you."[xliv][xlv] She whispered, "Thank you, Abba."

As she continued to dance in the circle, the instructor shouted, "Good job, McKnight! Did your two older brothers teach you that too?" and he chuckled.

She smiled and danced to the edge of the circle. "No, Sir! King David[xlvi] and Mary, Mary did, Sir!"

He shook his head. "I'm not even going to pretend to understand that, McKnight, but good work."

Chapter 29

Graduation

The next week flew by, Arabic language studies, weight training three times a week, a daily three-mile run, plus other classes and assessments. She accepted each challenge with diligence and endurance.

At last, on Graduation Day, the whole family crowded into the helicopter and Max flew them, including his beloved granddaughter Maddy and his great granddaughter Candy-E, to Quantico for Shayla's graduation. "It's a little tight, in here, but on the way home it will be more comfortable with the boys riding back with Special Agent Kitten."

They arrived on the tarmac to be greeted by Jager. "Welcome to Quantico. I'm Security Officer Jager, I've been commissioned by graduating Trainee McKnight to greet her family and offer you some refreshments before the ceremony."

Ashton stepped forward. "Thank you very much!" he turned, "And Mom, this is the Security Guard who came to Shayla's rescue when she was attacked by the guy with the knife."

Mom stepped closer, Jager extended his right hand, but Candice pushed it aside and surrounded him with a hug. "Thank you, young man for coming to the aid of my daughter, you're an angel."

He stood frozen, his face flashed red. "Thank you, ma'am."

Ashton tapped her on the shoulder. "Easy, Mom, let the man breath."

Everyone chuckled.

She stepped back. "I'm so sorry. Please forgive me."

Jager tipped his head down and with a sheepish

grin said, "That's okay ma'am, I'd love to have a mother like you and I think your daughter is terrific, stubborn, but terrific. I'd marry her tomorrow if I were allowed, but I've not even been given permission to take her on a date."

Mican laughed, "Yep, that's our sister okay."

Jager led them to The Clubs and seated them in the Families-Visitors Area, he swept his hand, "The facilities are over here. Please make yourselves comfortable until time for the ceremony, at which time, I'll escort you to your seats for graduation."

At the ceremony, Mican sat with his arm around Maddy, who cradled Candy-E in her arms, Max sat on her other side. Ashton sat next to Bailey with his arm around her shoulders and her hands folded atop her growing belly. Tom and Candice surveyed their brood of Chick-a-dees.

Candice kissed his cheek. "Oh, Thomas, I'm so very happy. You've brought such wonder into my life!"

The crowd was called to attention over the loud

speaker. "Ladies and Gentlemen, please stand for the National Anthem."

A WINDOW IN TIME

Chapter 30

Their Newest Agent

Shayla emerged from the crowd with her arms spread wide. "Mom, Dad, it's so good to see you! I've missed you all more that you'll ever know." She delivered an enormous hug for each of them.

Maddy stepped forward. "Here's the newest member of the family and she wants to meet her Auntie Shay."

Looking into the face of the baby, Shayla's knees almost buckled. "Mican, Maddy, she's beautiful! Can I hold her?"

Maddy placed the baby in Shayla's outstretched arms. "Oh, my goodness, I never knew how awesome this felt, holding new life and loving it so much." Tears weld up in her eyes.

Bailey waddled up. "Now mine. You can't hold him, but you can pat my belly."

Shayla handed Candy-E back to Maddy and wrapped her arms around Bailey's enormous form. "Oh, Bailey, you look wonderful!"

"Yeah, Shay-girl, sure! Like I'm fat and bulging."

Shayla backed up and started into Bailey's face. "You've never looked more beautiful, Bay, I'm so happy for you."

Max moved in. "Come here, girl, give me a hug."

Shayla reached up to wrap her arms around his enormous shoulders. "Thanks for getting everyone here, Uncle Max."

He pushed her back. "Speaking of looking good, you look great, Kitten."

"That's Special Agent Kitten to you, mister."

He leaned forward and slapped his knees, then he stood erect and saluted. "Yes, ma'am, Special Agent Kitten, now let's go to the luncheon."

Her brothers flanked her on either side as they walked to the dining area.

Mican asked first. "Do you have your assignment yet, sis?"

She glanced to the side. "No, not yet."

Ashton bellowed. "What? You don't know your assignment? The people who put your name forward haven't stepped up yet with an offer?"

She glanced to him. "Not yet, but keep your voice down. I'll fill you both in on our drive home. I don't want to spoil Mom's day."

Ashton leaned in and whispered, "What do you mean you don't want to spoil Mom's day, you didn't fail, or they wouldn't have graduated you, so what's up?"

Shayla smiled. "Later, gator, you'll have to wait." She zipped forward and hooked her wrists in Mom's and Philly's arms.

Chapter 31

Long Drive Home

Unlike their hour stuck in traffic around the base the day of their arrival at Quantico, the police held traffic for graduation attendees to exit. That helped to speed them on their way and at least they weren't leaving at rush hour.

Mican settled behind the steering wheel of the fully packed car, they exited the base with the rest of the traffic. "Well, Special Agent, Sergeant Kitten Copper Sister, what can you tell us, now that Mom and the rest of the family are on their way home with Max? What would've spoiled Mom's day?"

"I didn't want Mom to know yet that I may not be for home long. You know how they usually give you a packet with your assignment in it before graduation?"

Ashton leaned forward with his hands on the back of her seat. "Yeah, so what did yours say?"

"Mine was an invitation to attend the twenty-two-week, U.S. Marshal's Training Academy in Glynco, Georgia, starting right after the first of January."

"Wow! And you still don't know who initiated the request to have you invited to attend the FBI Academy?"

"I think, because I've now been invited to the U.S. Marshal's school, I have an idea. I think Philly and Max were right to say it was related to my adventure in helping to rescue kids when I was seventeen.[xlvii] One of the main guys that kept showing up was a Deputy U.S. Marshal Johnson. When I landed on the slave-trade ship, he was notified and he asked the Coast Guard Captain to detain any young female who was trying to rescue the trafficked kids, until he could get there. I had popped in and out of so many situations, I finally told him about Abba moving me into these places. Even though he already knew Abba, I had to lead him through a portal that hopped us from the trafficking ship to the Coast Guard boat. Needless to say, that convinced him that I was telling the truth about portals."

Mican glanced to the side. "So, are you going to accept the invitation? I mean are you going to go to the Marshal training course?"

"If I want to be in the new Cease and Desist Program, I guess I have to, she folded her arms and the tone of her voice changed, "but it's very frustrating not being able to talk directly to the people involved."

Chapter 32

Home

The drive home lasted about ten hours, but with the time change from Eastern to Central, they walked through the door at nine o'clock and just being home refreshed them.

Everyone had waited for their arrival.

The house glowed with lights from the sparkling Christmas tree in the corner by the fireplace, presents rested one atop another, filling the space underneath the tree. As what had become her new normal, Mom leapt into entertaining mode. "Is anyone hungry?"

Bailey sat up on the couch and stretched. "There's my dreamboat, welcome home, baby."

Everyone moved in for hugs.

Sandwiches and drinks were passed to the

ravenous group.

Shayla placed her arm around her mother. "Mom, the house looks so beautiful and the tree is stunning this year. What made you change to white roses and white satin bows?"

"I'm not sure, honey. It just felt right in my spirit somehow."

She hugged her mom. "Well you did an amazing job."

The family munched and chatted until almost midnight.

Mom suggested, "Since it's so late, would everyone like to spend the night? I'll get Tom to blowup air mattresses."

Maddy and Bailey, each nodded to their hubby.

Maddy added, "Candy-E is asleep in Ash's old room and I'd rather not move her, if it's okay with you, Mican."

"Sure babe," he hugged her, "it's good to be home, well at least be with you and Candy-E at my old home," he smiled.

Mom moved to direct traffic. "Shayla, we'll get

your stuff from the car tomorrow, for now, I know you're tired, so head to your room to bed."

"Mom, why don't you give Mican and Maddy his old room, they can open the extender door that use to make Ash's room[xlviii] and let Candy-E sleep in the pack-n-play where she is now. Ash and Bailey can have my room and I can sleep on the floor next to the Christmas tree." She cast a glance toward the couch. "Uncle Max can have the sofa, if he promises not to snore too loud."

Candice tipped her head. "Are you sure you'll be okay sleeping on the floor, Shay? I don't want you to be miserable now that you're back home."

"I'll be fine, Mom, it'll remind me of my rock-hard bed at Quantico," she winked at Max, "and I can race Uncle Max to the breakfast table in the morning."

"Okay, if you're sure." Mom looked around to see that everyone had fanned out to their respective sleeping areas. She laughed. "Well, they didn't take much convincing."

Shayla grabbed a pillow and a throw from the

recliner.

Candice glanced at Shayla and Max. "Are you two sure you'll be okay?"

"Yes, ma'am, goodnight!" She stretched out on the floor by the tree and as her mother turned her back, Shayla shook a package.

Mom swung around. "Okay you rascal, no repeat performances from childhood."

Shayla laughed. "Yes, ma'am and it's so good to be home. I love you, Momma."

"Love you too, my sweet girl."

Max stretched out on the sofa with a pillow and a throw, his socked feet stuck out slightly. "Goodnight, Special Agent Kitten."

"Goodnight, Uncle Max."

Chapter 33

The Next Morning!

Mom tried to be quiet in the kitchen, but she couldn't stop herself from humming Christmas carols.

Shayla heard the joyful voice and got up. She tiptoed into the kitchen and whispered, "Morning, Momma."

"Oh sweetie, I'm sorry I woke you. I tried to be quiet, but I'm so happy to have everyone here. This is going to be the most amazing Christmas ever, I feel it in my spirit!"

At breakfast, Shayla scanned the faces of the chattering group. Their numbers, had swollen to nine, now that Candy-E had been born and thanks to

Ashton and Bailey, number ten was on his way. Shayla prayed to herself, *Abba, when I was eleven, you showed me a picture of myself as an adult, a husband with a child stood behind me, you told me it would be a little while before I had my family,[xlix] but it's been so long. The boys each married at age twenty-six and I'll be twenty-seven tomorrow, how much longer before I meet my future husband? I've tried to be patient, but all I see before me is school and a career. I don't mean to complain, I loved my career as a police officer, I loved my time at the FBI Academy, but now more school looms before me. When, Lord, when?*

"Honey," Mom's voice broke her train of thought, "you haven't told us what your assignment will be, now that you've graduated from Quantico."

"I was waiting, Mom."

"Waiting for what, Chick-a-dee?"

"I didn't want to spoil your Christmas."

Candice's back straightened. "How could your assignment possibly spoil my Christmas?"

With her wrists resting on the table, Shayla

glanced around the table at her family. "I've been invited to attend the U.S. Marshals Training Academy."

Candice relaxed. "Why did you think that would spoil my Christmas, sweetie?"

"It's for twenty-two weeks in Glynco, Georgia, southeast of Atlanta, on the coast and I'll have to leave January second to drive there and arrive on time."

Candice smiled. "But it's so much closer, maybe you can come home for a visit mid-way through, honey."

Mican joined in. "I didn't know when to announce my news either, but I'll have to leave too, on January second. I'll be flying to Jordan to join the Copper Scroll project.

Watching his wife's face, Tom spoke-up. "Candice, we can discuss all this later, for now, let's enjoy our time with the kids and start our plans for Christmas."

Bailey leaned on the table. "Yeah, Shay-girl, tonight everyone is coming to our house for a

Christmas party. You haven't seen our new place."

Shayla lurched toward the table and faced Bailey. "You moved?"

"Yeah, Ash-boat found this cute little three-bedroom house near the zoo," she winked, "and he wanted us to move before the baby was born. We wanted it to be a surprise for everyone, but of course," she glanced around, "everyone wanted to help us move in, so you're the only one who hasn't seen it yet, but tonight you get the grand tour."

Chapter 34

Their New Home

Ashton stood in front of a picture window and watched the snow fall outside on the patio. The doorbell rang.

Candice and Tom sat on the couch, Bailey called from the kitchen. "Mom, would you mind answering that?"

She stepped into the little entryway and opened the front door. Mican and Maddy stood on the porch. Candice rubbed her hands together. "Come in here and give me that delicious baby."

Ashton turned to watch the scene unfold.

They stepped inside and Maddy placed Candy-E into her grandmother's arms. Mican removed his jacket and reached to help his wife take off her coat, then hung them both in the closet just inside the foyer. Candice cautiously returned to the living room and sat next to her husband, cuddling their first grandchild.

The doorbell rang again. Mican turned to open it. Shayla stood on the porch with her shoulders pulled tight to her ears and snow in her hair. "I thought Virginia was cold, but it's freezing here."

Mican reached to brush the snow off of her. "Come in, Sis and give me your coat, I'll hang it up." He pointed into the living room. "Mom and Philly are in there holding Candy-E and Ash has a fire roaring in the fireplace. Go on in and get warm."

Shayla gave him a hug. Maddy stood at the back of the sofa watching Candice and Tom with the baby. Shayla hugged her and stepped around to give her mom and dad a hug and kiss, when she approached Ashton for a hug, the teasing commenced. "Hey Shay, it's good to see you, and did Bailey tell you that we've decided on a name for the baby?"

She clamped her hands together in front of her

chest and smiled. "No, she didn't! What is it?"

"We've going to name him Sebastian."

"No way, you *are* not! You know I've said for years that if I had a boy, I'd name him Sebastian."

"Well, our guy can be Sea-bass-one and yours can be Sea-bass-two."

"You are not going to call my son Sea-bass-anything."

Bailey entered from behind her. "He's yanking your chain, Shay-girl, we're going to name him Ashby." She handed a tray of snacks to her husband.

Shayla placed her hands on her cheeks. "Ashby, that's so cute!"

"Thanks, we tried to follow the family tradition, so—Ash—for Ashton and the *b-y* are the first and last letters of Bailey, so—Ashby."

"I love it! Think about it, my niece and nephew are Candy-E and Ashby." She clasped her hands in front and hopped around. "I love it, I love it, I love it!"

Candice laughed. "Come here and love on your niece."

Shayla dashed past Mican and to her mom, as he headed for Ashton.

Mican laughed. "Look at the Special Agent Sergeant, she's such a kitten."

The doorbell rang again, but opened without help, Max shouted, "Merry Christmas! my lovely family."

Shayla now held Candy-E. "Come in Great Grandpa! Look who I've got."

Ashton still standing in front of the window. "Mican, look around, does this look familiar?"

Mican scanned the scene. "Hmmm, it does look familiar, but …"

His brother poked his shoulder. "Look at the window."

Mican turned and one hand came up to stroke his chin. "Yeah?"

Ashton leaned toward him and patted his chest. "This is my picture that Abba showed me when we were in the garden. Me, standing here in front of the picture window, snow falling outside, a fire in the fireplace, loving people filling the room, this is the fulfilment of my last picture. I didn't know it when I bought the house, but this place just felt right. Shayla's is the only," he signed air quotes, "final picture left to be fulfilled."

Bailey walked over and sighed. "Hmmm, fine host you are, give me that tray." She took the snacks from him and walked toward the sofa.

Mican chuckled. "Yep loving people all around."

Ashton laughed. "Most of the time I can't scrape her off of me, it must be the pregnancy hormones."

Mican punched his arm. "It could be that she wanted you to pass the snacks around and you didn't."

They both laughed and walked to the middle of the room where everyone chatted happily.

Candice stood and announced. "Remember, tomorrow night is at our house for Shayla's birthday."

Mican took Candy-E from his sister. "Mom what are you giving Shayla for her birthday?" He smiled. "Maddy and I have given her a niece."

Bailey chimed in. "Yeah, we're giving her an

Ashby, but she'll have to wait a little bit longer."

Max chirped in. "I'll give her a helicopter ride. I want her to see the changes in the valley since she's been away."

Mom stared lovingly at her daughter. "Well, we have a major surprise for her, but she'll have to wait until dinner tomorrow night for it."

Chapter 35

Shay's Birthday!

"Mom, can't you give me a hint about what you and dad are giving me for my birthday? And why do I have to wait until dinner? Is it a new car?"

"Nope?"

"Is it a new hand gun?"

Her stepdad on the sofa turned. "Heaven's no, Shayla, you already have more firearms than I do."

Having so much fun, Mom laughed. "It's something you've always wanted and you've never had before."

Shayla's nose crinkled and forehead wrinkled. "A horse?"

Mom giggled. "Nooooo, silly."

She scratched her head. "Are you getting me an apartment at the new complex down highway twenty-eight, near the church? Are you tired of me living with you?"

Mom whirled around with a huge grin on her face and a twinkle in her eyes. "You'll just have to wait, my dear."

"Do Mican and Ash know what it is?"

Philly answered. "That's a negatory."

"Do Bailey and Maddy know what it is?"

Mom tossed her head back and laughed. "No, it wouldn't be a secret for long if those two knew."

"Hmmm, so I'll get my surprise before dinner and," she paused and shouted "does Max know?"

Tom fell over on the couch laughing. "No, it would have been in the newspaper by now if he'd known."

Candice leaned over the back of the couch and eyed her husband with a scowl. "That's enough out of you, mister." She faced her daughter. "And no more questions from you, young lady."

Shayla pondered, *it's something I've always*

wanted, it's not a car or apartment, she chuckled to herself, *it's not a horse and the others don't know what it is.* She gasped aloud, but kept her thought to herself. *They're buying me a house! Mican has one, Ashton has one ... Something I've always wanted but never had. It must be a house!*

Her mother interrupted her train of thought. "Shay would you like to do some Christmas shopping today?"

"That's a great idea, Mom, but there aren't many places to shop in Sallis except Wally World, maybe I can just give promises and buy gifts after Christmas. We can go to a bigger town then."

"If that's what you want, that'll be fine."

For lunch they had sandwiches and chips. "Mom, this isn't much of a birthday celebration."

Candice smiled. "Shush! Now go get a shower and fix your hair and makeup. The others will be here for dinner and I want pictures. Make yourself fabulous for me and wear your blue dress." Candice kissed her daughter on the forehead. "Now shoo, go get ready, I have to set up for dinner."

She turned to face the direction of her room, but could see out the kitchen window. "Where's Philly going?"

"He's going to town to pick up some chicken and a cake from the Cookie Jar."

"Oh, my goodness, I've missed their fried chicken," she groaned, "and their fried catfish and hushpuppies."

"I'm trying to fix all your favorites, Maddy's favorites, Bailey's favorites, and as long as we have food, it'll be the boys' and Max's favorites."

They both laughed and Shayla nodded. "That's the truth."

"Now scram, sweetie, Max wants to take you for a flight just before sunset. He wants you to see the valley and the sky as the sun goes down, that's his present to you."

"Shouldn't I wait until we get back to put on the blue dress?"

"No, I'm afraid the others might be here when you get back, so go get ready now."

Slightly after three o'clock Max arrived and

shouted, of course for Max, his normal tone of voice could be mistaken for a shout. "Does anyone need a ride to the airport?"

Shayla stepped into the living room.

His eyes popped open wide and his head pulled back. "Wow, Kitten, you look spectacular!"

She looked down and smoothed her dress with her hands. "A little overdone for a family birthday party, don't you think?"

The flash of his teeth showed his approval, but he said, "Whatever your mom says, is fine with me, as long as I'm invited for dinner."

In the kitchen, Candice laughed and stepped into the living room. "That goes without saying Max, now let me see my daughter."

Shayla turned.

Her mother's mouth opened and she drew in a deep breath. "Oh Shayla, you're ... you're gorgeous."

She glanced down. "I think the dress is too tight, don't you?"

Her mother took her by the shoulders and turned

her around. "No, darling, it's just right. You've been wearing your sweats since you got home, so I hadn't realized what a dramatic difference five months at FBI school had made in you. No, it's not too tight, this is the way the dress was always supposed to fit, you just always wore your clothes too loose before," she chuckled, "this dress used to look like a sack on you."

Shayla placed her hands on her waist and cocked one hip to the side "Then why did you suggest I wear it?"

Candice giggled. "I thought the color would look good on you, but my goodness, you've turned into a lovely young woman." She looked into her daughter's eyes. "Now, you and Max skedaddle." She turned to their friend. "Max have her back on time for her surprise."

Max saluted. "Yes, ma'am, Momma Hen."

They walked to the driveway, Max helped Shayla into the jeep and drove to the air field where he assisted her into the helicopter. "Sergeant Kitten Copper Special Agent, you used to could hop in here without a problem."

"It's this darn dress, it's too tight."

Max chuckled. "Darlin' you used to be a tomboy, so having a dress that fits properly feels strange to you, but I gar-ran-tee that it looks fab. Now, let's go see the sights, you're gonna see 'em like you've never seen 'em before." He pulled back on the cyclic collective and they rose slowly, headed forward and angled toward town.

As he banked around the north end of town, Shayla leaned toward the door, her seatbelt pulled tight. "Uncle Max, why haven't you ever offered to teach any of us to fly?"

"Well, Kitten, I didn't know any of you wanted to learn. No one ever asked and just having Maddy and you and your brothers in my life was more than I ever dreamed of, I didn't want to be pushy, but if you want to learn, it would be my pleasure to teach you."

"Thanks, Uncle Max, I'd love to learn, but now it'll have to wait until after Marshal's school."

He glanced at her. "So, you're going to accept the

invitation?"

"I guess so, but," she sighed, "it feels like that's all my life has been, one school after another: elementary school, junior high, high school, then college, the police academy, then Quantico, now the Marshals Academy."

A rumble of laughter broke her solemn mood.

She scowled at him.

Max continued to laugh. "So, you think that's what it's been, so far? Have you forgotten that not every pretty young woman has time-traveled, helped break-up a secret underground base of bad guys, rescued kidnapped kiddos, been a copper and gone to Quantico? Honey, you're just in a funk. What's the matter?"

"I'm sorry, Uncle Max, but Mom has Philly, Mican has Maddy and Candy-E, Ash has Bailey and Ashby on the way," her eyes cut over to him and smiled, "and you've got all of us, but I don't have anyone special."

"Oh Kitten, you're just in a slump between exciting adventures, that always happened to me at the end of an assignment, everything seems so humdrum because you're use to the action, the challenge and excitement," he grinned at her and pointed, "now, hush up and look down there, there's your house."

She leaned to the window and looked out, just as a new car pulled into the driveway. She nodded. "So, my present *is* a new car, I wonder why they didn't just tell me?"

Max angled the copter westward. "Look out there at that sunset."

She squinted and grabbed her sunglasses. "Wow, that's spectacular."

Max laughed. "Then that makes two of you!"

She glanced at him and smiled.

"We'd better head home, or your momma 'll have my guts for garters."

He landed the chopper, they climbed out and strolled to the jeep, got in and drove back up the mountain to the house.

They arrived at dusk, the dark sedan was the only

car on the driveway.

"Kitten, I'm going to wait out here for Maddy and the others. Tell your momma I'll come in when they arrive.

She darted to the new car and glanced through the window into the front seat, "I like the color," then dashed to the house and threw the door open, but before she could blurt out anything about the car, a man rose from the end of the sofa and turned to face her. She stopped in her tracks, speechless.

With a smile that lit the room, the man said, "Hello Shayla, do you remember me?"

Her mouth dropped open and her arms dangled at her sides. "Beau, what on earth are you doing here?"

Mom stepped forward and handed her a letter. "Read this, honey, it will explain everything."

Tom Phillips rose and stood beside his wife, his arm around her waist.

With her mouth still ajar, Shayla took the well-worn letter and read.

Dear Miss McKnight,

Today, we met for the first time, though you will not receive this letter for ten years, but in order for you to understand (when I am finally able to present this to you) I will attempt to explain.

Shayla, I have been a Christian since I was ten-years-old. About a year after my commitment to the Lord, Abba showed me pictures of myself as an infant, then as a child, all the way to manhood.

In the final picture, Abba showed me a beautiful lady probably in her early thirties. I was standing behind her holding a small child. At that time, he told me I would have a family, but *it would be a little while* and I was to be patient and to wait.[1]

When I met you today, or ten years ago, I instantly recognized you as the lady in the picture, but then to my amazement I learned you were only seventeen. Abba's words, *it would be a little while,* rang in my heart.

In prayer, I sought his guidance. The Lord assured me we would meet again, ten years from today. Though I was twenty-one at the time, he asked me to wait and to save myself for you and that you would do the same for me. He told me to pursue my career, but that he also had a plan for your life; so patiently, I have endeavored over the years to keep an eye on you and your career from afar.

I trust the Lord so much that I will wait/have waited for you. Even at age seventeen, Shayla, you are (were) the most remarkable young woman I've ever known. Your devotion to and trust of Abba was amazing. Your dedication to the children you were attempting to rescue was inspiring. Your fierceness in battle was moving, but to learn of your power in spiritual warfare was thrilling.

You were quite beautiful then, but you won my heart with your virtue; your beauty was only enhanced by your nobility of heart. You are truly unique and I am convinced you are the only girl/woman in the world for me.

Shayla McKnight, will you look away from this letter—at me down on one knee—and will you accept my proposal of marriage?

Your Hopeful Future Partner in Life,

Beau Johnson[li]

The paper fell to her side, gripped in one hand, her mouth still slightly open, she saw Beau on one knee, holding a ring, with the tips of his index finger and thumb.

"Shayla, I've asked your parents' permission and they've given it. Will you marry me?"

Still speechless, she stood there. Finally regaining the ability to speak, she snapped, "Without a word to me all these years? You let me think that I was a fool for loving you."

His head tipped forward and his eyes stared at the floor. "Please don't be mad. I wanted you to follow the path Abba had chosen for you." He looked back at her. "At Abba's direction, I formed a committee of people who had met you ten years ago when you were rescuing kids and we submitted your name to an FBI department head and requested that you be invited to Quantico, in the hope that you would do well, which I was sure you would, then you could attend the Marshals Academy and at the conclusion, you could join me in the FBI's and Marshal's newly forming joint task force. I wanted to give you that letter this past summer, but I didn't want to be in the way of you accepting or rejecting the invitation to Quantico, and to be honest, I wasn't sure if I would be able to wait, if I got that close to you, so I waited and stayed anonymous. I only wanted what was best for you, please don't be angry."

She folded her arms and one foot slid out to the side.

"Shayla, when I met you, Abba asked me to wait. He told me we would meet again in ten years. If I had defied that and say, I waited five years and approached you when you graduated from college, I believe you would have accepted my proposal and you would've married me and taken some puttering, little job. I believe you would've been happy and so would I, but *you,* Shayla would never have been a Police Officer, you would never have gone to Quantico, you would not have the physical experiences and power that you have now. You would not be as spiritually strong as you are now, you would have had me, but you would have been less than half of what you are today, half of what God wanted you to be."

Her fists hopped to her waist. "So why now, Beau?"

He stood to face her. "Because I'll be one of the faculty members at the Marshals Academy and if you decide to attend, I'll have to declare our relationship and make sure that you're not in any of my classes."

"Why would that matter?"

He reached for her hand. "Because if we're in a relationship, you won't be allowed in any of my classes, in order to prevent favoritism, but we can still see each other in the evenings and on weekends when you're not studying, that will give you time to get to really know me and to decide if you really want to marry me," he lifted her hand and kissed it, "but Shayla McKnight, you're the only woman I've ever loved in the thirty-one years of my life and I don't want to have to live another day without you. Will you please marry me?"

She jerked her hand from his.

His eyes flew open wide.

She tiptoed and flung her arms around his neck. "Yes, yes, yes, a thousand times yes."

He lifted her feet from the floor, hugging her for all of the times over the past ten years that he'd craved to hold her. "Shayla, I love you." He set her feet back on the floor.

She pushed away. "I've loved you since I was seventeen. I tried to tell myself it was a silly schoolgirl crush, but Beau, I love you too, with all my heart and when I was eleven, Abba had shown me a picture of myself as a mature woman about thirty with a tall man standing behind me holding a small child, but their faces were blurred."

He tossed his head back and laughed. "It's exactly the same picture he showed me when I was eleven, but your face was as clear as day, I knew it was you the minute I saw you, but what a shock to learn that you were only seventeen. I assure you, that took a lot of praying and restraint, and the child you saw in my arms will be a boy with curly blonde hair."

Staring up into Beau's charming face and mesmerizing eyes surrounded by his lush, dark eyelashes, she said, "And his name will be Sebastian, if that's okay with you?"

He lifted her hand, kissed it again and slid the ring onto her finger. "Sebastian Johnson, that sounds great to me, my love."

Mom clasped her hands in front of her, tears streaking down her cheeks. "Honey, Beau called us two days ago to see if he could come talk to us. Since you've mentioned him a few times over the years, we thought just having him here would be a nice birthday surprise. We assumed his visit had to do with the invitation to the Marshals Academy, then he mentioned that he would like to propose, if we approved after meeting him. We were blown away, but so blessed by his humble obedience to Abba that we could never have said no."

Shayla laughed. "So, when I asked if Max knew what my surprise was, Philly, that's why you said he would have put it in the newspaper by now if he'd known."

Tom wrapped his arm around Candice, but spoke to his stepdaughter. "Yep, I think Max will be as thrilled as we are and Shayla," he smiled at her, "if you hadn't accepted Beau's proposal, I think I would have spanked you for the first time in our relationship."

Shayla burst out laughing. "I've never told you two about my crush on Beau, due to the fact that I thought it was foolish because of the age difference," she stopped and her head tipped slightly to the side, "which doesn't seem to be such a big deal now and because," her face flashed hot, "he's so handsome." She cut her eyes up to meet his.

Car doors slammed on the driveway.

"Oh, my goodness, the kids are here for your birthday dinner." Mom wiped her face and patted Shayla on the arm and smiled up at Beau. "I'll let you two decide how to break the news to everyone." Mom rushed to the door.

Beau bent to Shayla's ear. "May I kiss you?"

She smiled and nodded.

He faced her, lifted her chin and kissed her, just

as the door opened.

Bailey, Ashton, Maddy holding Candy-E, Mican and Max stood on the porch and gasped.

Bailey shouted, "Who's the hunk kissing Shay-girl?"

Following the kiss, with a smile from ear-to-ear, Shayla stepped to his side and wrapped her arms around his waist to face her family. "Everybody, this is Beau."

Ashton whispered to his brother, "Dude, look at him. You know, bro, we're not bad looking guys, but he looks like he should be on the cover of a men's magazine and he's at least two inches taller than you are, is he for real?"

Mican laughed. "I want to know where he came from?"

Ashton whispered again. "You know, he's that U.S. Marshal, remember Shay talking about 'Beau this' and 'Beau that'?"

Oblivious to what was going on around them, Beau bent to Shayla's ear again. "Happy Birthday, my darling."

As her family walked in, Shayla whispered something to Beau, he smiled and nodded.

Everyone gathered around the couple to greet the new boyfriend, but Shayla looked at her parents. "Mom, I'll be tied up at the Marshals Academy for a while, would you mind starting to plan a wedding for around the third or fourth week of this coming June?"

Mouths dropped open.

Bailey shouted. "What in the freakin' daylights just happened here?"

Chapter 36

Two Days Before Christmas

Beau had been invited to spend Christmas with the family, so he and Shayla walked on the mountain and strolled through town to get to know each other better without the stress of Portal Travel or rescuing kids.[lii] Shayla decided to take him to meet her former coworkers at the local Police Department. When she walked in a cheer went up.

Chief Hansen stepped from his office to see what the commotion was all about.

Shayla made the introductions. "Chief Hansen, this is Assistant Chief Deputy U.S. Marshal Beau Johnson."

The chief looked up at him, stretched out his hand

and smiled. "So, Assistant Chief Deputy U.S. Marshal, are you the yahoo who took our favorite Sergeant from us?"

Beau returned the smile and accepted the chief's hand. "Sir, it's nice to meet you and I'm only responsible for contacting some people that Sergeant McKnight had met several years ago and asking if they would like to put her name forward for Quantico. She's responsible for the rest of the story."

"Well, Deputy, you took the best officer that ever graced the Police Force here in Sallis, Tennessee."

Beau's eyes shifted to Shayla. "She's definitely one-of-a-kind, Sir."

Shayla lifted her left hand. "I have some more news for you, Chief."

His eyes rested on the sparkling diamond, he looked at her and flashed a smile. "McKnight, what have you gone and done? I was hoping you'd come back here after Quantico and marry my son, or at least fulfill Martha's dream and marry Charlie."

People around the station chuckled and Stanley punched Charlie in the shoulder.

Beau took Shayla's hand, glanced over his shoulder, then back to Hansen. "Sorry Chief, I've had my heart set on this one for a long time, but I was waiting for God to give the okay."

The Chief folded his arms. "McKnight, you never even gave us an inkling of an idea that you had a guy."

She chuckled. "Truthfully, Chief, I never knew he wanted me, but now," she scanned the room, "you're all invited to the wedding."

Beau turned to the men in the squad room. "Did you officers know that you'd been working with a hero? This young woman helped to rescue dozens of people who were being trafficked, from young children to a group of farm workers who were being used as forced labor. She personally helped reunite two kids with their mothers and she was only seventeen at the time. I hope that you took note of her character and her dedication, you'll never find a better role model."

Whispers of, "seventeen," and "hero," went up across the room before the officers stood and clapped, then each stepped forward to congratulated the couple.

Stanley Marcum took Shayla's hand and leaned to her ear. "I'm sorry for all the teasing and harassment I gave you, will you please forgive me, Sarge?"

She nodded, smiled and whispered, "You're forgiven, Stanley."

Following their visit to the police station, they decided on lunch at the Cookie Jar Café which turned into a feast.

The hostess came to seat them.

Beau asked, "Do you have a small table in the back corner?"

They were shown to the table, seated and given menus.

Glancing over the list of offerings, Beau asked, "Shayla have you ever tried their steaks?"

"One time I had a ribeye and it was delicious."

Beau chuckled. "I should have known, ribeye is my favorite steak too."

The waitress approached. "Hey, Shayla, welcome back. Are you going to rejoin the police force?"

Shayla lifted her left hand and smiled. "No, I have other plans."

The girl flashed a smile at Beau. "Congrats, you guys. What can I get you for lunch?"

"Ma'am, we'll have two ribeye steaks."

"How do you want 'em cooked?"

Beau glanced at Shayla. "Medium rare for mine."

He laughed. "That will be two, medium rare steaks with baked potatoes." He glanced at Shayla.

She nodded, *yes*.

"With sour cream and butter, plus two tossed salads with ... Ranch Dressing?"

Shayla laughed. "What else for a Texas boy and a country girl."

"And what would y'all like to drink?"

They both nodded and said, "Sweet tea."

Shayla added, "And please hold the bread until our meal comes out. I don't want to fill up on your homemade rolls and iced tea, like I usually do." She smiled at the waitress.

"Yes, ma'am and I'll throw in a couple of our Wedding Cake cupcakes for dessert, on the house."

After lunch, Beau and Shayla drove to the bluff overlooking Sallis. On the way, he opened his heart to her. "Shayla, it's been so difficult staying away from you, especially this last year."

She shifted in her seat to face him. "Was that you, after my promotion last July, across from the Mexican restaurant, in the shade?"

"Yes, that was me, I had hoped you wouldn't notice me, but when I saw you look across the street, I was afraid you'd recognized me, it looked like you were staring into my eyes."

She shook her head. "I saw a man, but in the shade and being that far away, I couldn't tell who it was, besides I never dreamed you'd be there, Beau."

"After the ceremony, when you were dismissed, so many people surrounded you, I knew I could get away, but I couldn't make myself leave, I stayed and watched as one after another, people spoke to you, I could tell how much they cared, then your stepdad and Max came and got you." A one-second glance met her eyes, but he focused again on the curvy road. "I've tried to stay away from you, but I desperately wanted to be there and watch your promotion ceremony, I tried to be more careful after that."

Her eyes opened wider. "After that? Where else did you show up?"

"Since I was already in town for your promotion, I followed you to the Cookie Jar."

"So that *was* you in the cowboy hat?" She looked in the backseat and there was the white Stetson, she smiled.

"Yeah, I tried to get away in such a hurry, I almost tripped over that small kids' table and little rocking chair by the stairs." He chuckled. "I guess I should brush up on my surveillance technique."

Shayla laughed. "Was that the last time you followed me?"

"I'm embarrassed to say, no, it wasn't, I stayed over to watch you leave for Quantico. I went to my room at the Mountain Inn,[liii] showered, checked out, then slept in my car that night, I dreamt about you standing next to me wearing a long white wedding dress with sheer sleeves. You were so lovely," he glanced at her, "you *are* so lovely, Shayla."

Her face felt warm, but she persisted. "Why did you sleep in your car, if you had a room?"

"I parked down the road from your house, so I wouldn't miss you leaving. I couldn't make myself go home, but I also couldn't run the risk of you changing your mind about going to Quantico. It already seemed like it was difficult for you to go."

She sighed and stared at her hands in her lap. "It was hard, Beau." All of a sudden, her face brightened, "but did you know, you creeped Mican out that morning, being parked down the road, he saw you sitting in your car, then he thought you ducked, what you don't know is that a few years ago, when we first moved here, we had a run-in with some bad guys who used to park down there and follow us. There's actually a secret underground base down where you were parked,[liv] but that's a story for another time." She giggled. "Okay, where else did you show up?"

"I followed you to Quantico and when you said goodbye to your brothers and Max on the tarmac, it broke my heart to see you standing there alone. I was on my way to get someone to go help you, when the archangel showed up, but I knew you were in good hands then."

Her head snapped to face him and her voice went up two octaves. "The archangel? You knew who Jager was?"

He laughed and teased. "Sure, didn't you?"

"Nooo, I didn't, but did you know a demon was stalking me?"

He turned a serious face to her, then his eyes back to the road. "Not until I prayed about it and Abba explained to me why Gabriel was assigned to you. At that moment, I had a choice, I could be afraid and rush to you, but I would be in disobedience and would be powerless. I would never have been able to keep you safe, or my other choice was, I could choose to trust Abba to fulfill his plan in our lives. I chose to trust the Lord, I prayed for you, then returned to my office in Texas, but I want you to know, there has never been a day since I met you ten years ago that you were not in my thoughts and prayers."

"Oh, Beau, I've thought about you every day since we met, I can't believe you felt the same way all those years. You amaze me with your strength, how will I ever be worthy of your love?"

"In some ways you've been stronger than I have, you've had to handle your love for me without ever seeing me and," he flashed a smile at her, "you don't have to do anything to be worthy of my love, Shayla, since I was eleven, I wanted you to be my wife. God placed a love and desire in me that only you can fill."

With her face now roasting hot, she changed the subject. "Okay, so are those the only times, let's say … you visited me, without me knowing?"

"No, of course not," he laughed, "I wanted to take you to your high school prom."

She bellowed with laughter. "Now that would have turned some heads." She giggled. "I would have loved to see their faces if I'd walked in on your arm."

He chuckled, "I know you went alone, Shayla, I'm so sorry for that, but you looked very pretty in your prom dress." He smiled. "Then of course, I returned for your high school graduation, your graduations from college and from the Police Academy, oh and I was at Mican's wedding and Ashton's, uninvited of course. I tried to see you about once a year, but other than that, no, I didn't visit you." He smiled at her and his gleaming white teeth captured her heart all over again.

"I can't believe you did all that for me."

His smile vanished and the corners of his mouth drooped. "I'm ashamed to say, I didn't do it for you, Shayla, I did it for me. I longed to be with you so much, those times were as close as I dared get, but to have stayed away completely would have been torture. At least this way, I could love you from a distance and share in your triumphs."

"Why didn't you at least call me and tell me that you thought about me?"

"Abba had told me it would be ten years before I met you again, so I tried to stay away. If I had made my love known to you before then, I don't think either of us could have waited, like I told you before, it would have robbed you of all the experiences you've had up to this point." They arrived at the crest of the mountain, he got out, walked around, opened her door and reached for her hand.

She placed her fingers in his open palm, stepped from the car and he tucked her hand in the bend of his arm. "Shayla, you will never know how many times I've wanted to call you, to text you, to hold you, but I knew I couldn't interfere in your life until Abba gave me permission, or it would've derailed his plans for both of our lives." He pointed to a bench on the edge of the cliff.

They walked the few steps, she turned to sit with her back to the view and stared up at him. "I'm sorry for how you've struggled, Beau. I understand now why Abba blurred your face in the image he showed me. I could never have been as strong or as obedient as you've been. Oh, Beau, I would lie in bed at night, a teenage kid and think about you, figuring you were out with some glamorous, sophisticated woman, having dinner and strolling in the park under the moonlight. You were then and still are the handsomest man I've ever seen," she stared at the ground, "and the kindest, most noble man I've ever known," she looked up again.

He held her chin, smiled and stared into her eyes.

"And that's no shallow admission, Beau. I've had examples in my life like my dad Michael, my stepdad Philly, and his friend Max, I never thought anyone could measure up to them, then you swept into my life like a superhero."

Beau laughed. "But without the cape."

She giggled. "No, it was with cowboy boots and a bola tie, you were so cute." Shayla looked down again. "The idea of being with you felt so impossible, I was so young, so plain, so ordinary, all I could do was to roll over and cry into my pillow because it hurt so bad not to be with you or even be able to tell you how I felt. As hard as I tried, I couldn't get you out of my heart or my mind. Do you know that I've never dated anyone else," her face heated up, "or romantically kissed anyone else?"

He knelt in front of her and their eyes met. "Shayla, when we met, you were so focused on, so dedicated to rescuing those people, I had no idea that you even remembered me, which broke my heart. I felt so hopelessly in love with you that all I could do was pray and trust Abba that my heart wouldn't burst," he lifted her fingers and kissed them, "and my dear, yes, you were young, but you were never ordinary, or plain, you were then and still are the most beautiful, extraordinary creature I've ever known. In my mind, I clung to the picture of me standing lovingly behind you, holding our son. I longed to see that picture, that promise, be fulfilled."

She opened her hand onto his cheek and brushed it back over his ear and hair.

He reached for her hand and kissed her palm. "And I've never had another woman, Shayla, since I was eleven-years-old, I knew your face and I waited for that face, I knew you were the only woman for me." He lifted her hand, kissing the scar on her wrist. "I see you escaped from the zip-ties," then his long eyelashes obscured his eyes from her view, as he kissed her hand.

All of a sudden, her hand jerked away from his lips, his eyes flew open and he watched as a menacing, shadowy figure drug Shayla backwards from the bench.

A cloud shrouded the sun, the icy winter wind whipped up the face of the mountain, swishing her long, lovely, hair behind her, her woolen coat, squished tight against her body. She screamed, "Beau!"

He lunged for the figure, but it drifted out past the edge of the cliff beyond his reach, he flailed his arms, managing to regain his balance. He yelled, "Stop! Give her to me."

The ominous dark cloud spewed a slur. "What is it worth to you, illegitimate son of John?"

Shayla struggled and shouted. "He is not illegitimate, he's a son of the King."

A grotesque laugh followed. "What then, oh child of the King? What will you wager for her life?"

Beau shouted. "My life, for hers!"

Shayla struggled in the grasp of the figure and

screamed. "No Beau, you can't do that, I love you!"

The cloud moved toward the edge and her feet dangled above the ground. The darkness stretched out to engulf Beau, but did not release Shayla.

She shouted, "Jager, I need you, where are you?"

Abba's voice answered. "Beau is your warrior now, pray for him."

In dismay and disbelief, Shayla writhed in the clutch of the specter.

Calm words came into her spirit. "Close your eyes, child, reach out in faith, not fear. Put your eyes on me and what I can do."

In obedience, her eye's clamped shut. "Abba, help Beau, help me."

"My dear child, feel me with your spirit, turn loose of the fear, fear is a weapon of the demon. Don't abide in fear, my child, abide in me."

The Holy Spirit came upon her with a calming touch. "Yes, Abba, what do I pray?"

"Pray that Beau reaches out with his spirit, he wrestles not against flesh and flood, but this one has an assignment from a ruler of darkness,[iv] it's purpose is to stop you both from entering into your destiny, from entering into a new arena of spiritual warfare like you've never known before. You and he will do great and mighty things in the days to come, but you must keep your eyes on me. Now, deal with this one in the spiritual realm, call for warriors."

"Heavenly Father, send your warring angels to fight this battle for Beau and for me, so that the picture of promise you showed each of us will be fulfilled. Give Beau this revelation too." She opened her eyes, to witness the man she loved struggling with the dark cloud that shifted and changed in shape and size. She forced her hands into the demonic cloud. Gritting her teeth, she growled. "By the Power of God and the blood of Jesus, I command you to take us back to the mountain top and release us." Her words rushed out as power.

Flashes of light hit the darkness, pushing it toward the top of the mountain.

As Beau wrestled, the figure grew smaller and Beau's voice rang out true and clear. "And you will *not* prevail over Shayla nor me." He punched the billowy darkness with his right fist. "We have a heavenly destiny to be together and you will not harm either of us." He punched with his left as he proclaimed, "You cannot cause us to be unproductive in the natural world nor in the spiritual realm, we will raise a family and our son will grow to be mighty warrior, you will never have me, nor Shayla, nor our son Sebastian, nor Shayla's family, nor Max, nor my mother. I decree it by legal authority, from the court of heaven,[lvi] as a son of God and in the mighty name of Jesus."

The cloud grew smaller and weaker as they neared the edge of the cliff.

Beau yelled, "In Jesus' name, be gone forever, you foul spirit!" And their feet thudded onto the rock.

Shayla melted into his arms. "Oh, Beau, I was so scared."

He kissed the top of her head. "I prayed for you my love, that you wouldn't be afraid and that you would fight in the spirit, then I heard your words 'send your warring angels,' I knew you would be fine and so would I." He pushed her away from his body and looked deep into her eyes. "You were afraid that you would lose me now that you finally know that I love you and I was afraid I would lose you now that I can hold you as my own, but you and I were never in danger of losing each other to the demon, we were only in danger of the fear causing us to take our eyes off of Abba," he lifted his palms to her cheeks, "but we pushed through, Shayla, we prevailed." He kissed her, pulled her to his chest and they stood there with their arms wrapped securely around each other for a long time. Finally, after their hearts slowed and beat as one, they returned to Shayla's home and informed her parents of the demonic encounter and knowing they should be together, they added a request to move up the wedding date.

Chapter 37

The Day After Christmas

With Christmas gifts opened and the litter cleared away, new packages adorned the hearth next to the tree. The living room furniture now waited on the back porch and twenty folding chairs, borrowed from the church, hosted guests in short, neat rows.

Ashton ran the digital video camera he'd borrowed from work, while Mican took still shots with his phone.

Everyone had gathered in their Christmas finery, including Benji, Holly, Chief Davis, his wife Samantha, Chief Hansen, all the crew from the day shift of the local police department, including the dispatcher, plus Charlie's mom Martha. Candy-E wore the red velvet dress her grandmother Candice had given her, of course it came with a red bow for her hair.

A bowl of punch and a silver foil tray holding a small two-layer, white frosted wedding cake, topped with two red rose buds, surrounded by two dozen chocolate cupcakes, all from the Cookie Jar, waited atop a lovely white, lace tablecloth on the dining room table, as snow floated down outside the picture window.

Max had flown to Texas on Christmas Day to bring Beau's mom into town, she beamed with pride at her son standing facing the group.

Tall and lean with broad shoulders, Beau struck a handsome figure in a plain black suit, white shirt, a sweet silver tie he'd borrowed from Mican and shiny black cowboy boots with silver tips on the toes. Behind him, the tree gleamed with its clear lights, white roses and white satin bows.

Thomas Phillips escorted his stepdaughter into

the living room.

A simple, long white dress with sheer sleeves flowed fluidly over Shayla's newly found curves. Bailey had fashioned her long hair into a soft upswept style with tendrils around her face, in her hands she held a white lace handkerchief, borrowed from her soon-to-be mother-in-law, she pressed it against the back of her white Bible, on top lay two red rose buds, whose stems were laced together with a blue satin ribbon.

Her stepdad whispered, "I'm sure your dad is pleased with your marriage, your mom and I are and I know Abba is." They continued down the aisle between the rows of chairs and he placed her hand in Beau's.

The pastor stood beside the Christmas tree with its glistening lights, while praise music played in the background. All-in-all, the simplest, yet most elegant wedding scene imaginable. "Dearly beloved, we are gathered here in the sight of God and these witnesses to join this man," the minister pointed his book toward Beau, "Beauregard Orville Johnson, and this woman," the book swung toward Shayla, "Shayla Marie McKnight, in holy matrimony. If anyone has any objection to this union, let them speak now or forever hold their peace." He scanned the crowd and his eyes rested on Charlie's mom.

Martha grinned, tucked her chin and shook her head *no*.

The pastor chuckled. "Looks like there aren't any objections."

He waited for the laughter to die down.

"Do you, Beau take this woman to be your lawfully wedded wife?"

He stared into Shayla's eyes, smiling, his white teeth gleaming. "With all my heart, I do!"

Bailey clapped and shouted, "Woohoo!"

After waiting for the laughter to subside again, he addressed Shayla. "Do you, Shayla take this man to be your lawfully wedded husband?"

Shayla returned Beau's loving gaze. "Yes, please."

Maddy and Bailey giggled.

Mom wiped tears from her face.

The minister gave his next instructions. "The ring is a symbol of your unending love, Beau, please place the ring on Shayla's finger."

He paused, then turned. "Shayla please place the ring, signifying your unending love for Beau on his finger."

Pausing again, he smiled at the couple and proclaimed, "I now pronounce you husband and wife, you may kiss the bride."

Cheers went up from all corners of the room.

Mom and Bailey stood and threw flower petals at the couple as they embraced in their first kiss as husband and wife. When their lips parted, they gazed into each other's eyes and smiled.

The pastor announced, "It's my great pleasure and honor to present to you, for the very first time, Mr. and Mrs. Beauregard Johnson."

Just the Beginning!

Hogan's Alley

In 1986, a catastrophic shootout on a Miami street saw a group of FBI agents try to stop suspected bank robbers; two were killed and another five were wounded.

Special agent in charge of the Miami FBI during the incident, Joseph Corless described it "a devastating day for the FBI."

From this tragedy came change, in this case the decision to invest in the mock town of Hogan's Alley to allow agents to gain experience they needed to avoid future tragedies, without getting hurt.

The fake township of Hogan's Alley, sits on a 60-acre FBI training facility near the small, real town of Quantico, Virginia. It was established using the expertise of Hollywood film set designers.

The buildings, or in most cases building fronts, were designed and built in order to create what the FBI describe as a "realistic urban setting for training FBI agents, DEA (Drug Enforcement Agency), and other local, state, federal and international law enforcements agents."

The township is equipped with all the essential amenities of any modern urban city — including a bank, hotel, laundromat, warehouses, shops, cinema, pool hall, deli, houses and of course, a bar — with many named after historical FBI events.

The township looks so realistic that a huge number of letters were actually posted there, filling up the Hogan's Alley only post box so often that it had to be welded shut.

But if you look a bit deeper you will discover that behind the Dogwood Inn Restaurant is an FBI classroom and the Manhattan Melodrama Theatre won't showcase your favorite performance.

Investigative techniques, surveillance, firearm skills, defensive tactics, investigations of terrorist activities, making arrests, gathering and processing evidence at crime scenes, conducting searches and interviews, even simulated gun fights with realistic paint ball guns are all part and parcel of Hogan's Alley.

One of the most advantageous aspects of the facility is that it allows for updated and new tactical techniques to be trailed and tested in a safe setting before being launched into a real-life scenario.

The faux criminal situations and environment also

allow for mistakes to take place and most importantly allow for opportunities to learn from them, before law enforcement head out into real life situations.

The neighboring, real town of Quantico, is bordered on three sides by one of the largest US Marine bases and it is from this community that local residents, often Marine family members, are recruited as actors for the many criminal activities occurring next door.

Taking on the part of criminal drug dealers or terrorists, or even as victims or bystanders, the actors are an essential part of the training program.

As well as being active in a mock live crime scene, they will also be arrested, interviewed and processed; the procedures are thorough and realistic. Sometimes the faux criminal will even resist arrest, setting up an unprecedented chase.

Once the active component is complete, they will then take part in the critique that follows each exercise to provide feedback and suggestions for improvement.

Hogan's Alley, whose name was taken from the 1800s comic strip, *Yellow Kid* was chosen because the fictional alley in the comic, Hogan's Alley, was located in a rough neighborhood, just like this fake crime town. Its name hasn't disappointed.

Now a term used to describe any tactical training ground, Hogan's Alleys have been a staple of training in the US since the 1920s and are now found in other countries around the world including Hogan's Alley that was established in Gravesend, England in 2003.

The crime and arrest capital of the US has allowed thousands of law enforcement members to effectively train for over three decades now. Its focuses have changed from mobsters and bank robbers to terrorist attacks and hostage scenarios, adapting to the needs of the society it is seeking to protect.

Hogan's Alley has been a hot bed of criminal activity for over 30 years and it seems it will continue to be so for years to come.

Shona Hendley is a freelance writer from Victoria. You can follow her on Instagram.[lvii]

June Whatley currently has three Christian Adventures available for kids ages @ 8-18. The Sleeper Awakens, Cloud Skimmers, and From the D.E.E.P.

She has taught first through third grades in a Christian school; she has also taught Middle Graders in two different Christian schools; and has taught Study Skills in the Remedial Developmental Department of the third largest college in Tennessee.

Mrs. Whatley holds a combination Master of Arts degree in Counseling and Education from Regent University in Virginia Beach, Virginia.

June is a wife, mother, grandmother of four of the greatest Grands in history, plus a doggie-momma to Bear and Millie.

Follow her on Amazon

Endnotes:

---

[i] *The Sleeper Awakens,* June Whatley, Jurnee Books, 2021, pp. 202-205.

[ii] *The Sleeper Awakens.*

[iii] *The Sleeper Awakens.*

[iv] *Whisked Away*, June Whatley, Jurnee Books, 2021.

[v] *Whisked Away.*

[vi] *The Sleeper Awakens, p.150.*

[vii] *From the D.E.E.P.,* June Whatley, Jurnee Books, 2021.

[viii] *Whisked Away.*

[ix] https://en.wikipedia,org>wiki>Qumran

[x] https://en.wikipedia.org/wiki/Copper_Scroll

[xi] https://en.wikipedia.org/wiki/Copper_Scroll

[xii] Cookie Jar Café, 1887 Kelly Cross Road, Dunlap, TN 37327. Yes, it's real.

[xiii] http://fbina1.blogspot.com/2014/11/getting-ready-to-go-what-to-bring.html

[xiv] *From the D.E.E.P.*

[xv] *From the D.E.E.P.*

[xvi] *Cloud Skimmers,* June Whatley, Jurnee Books, 2021.

[xvii] https://www.google.com/search?client=safari&rls=en&q=is+there+a+difference+between+an+FBI+special+agent+and+an+agent&ie=UTF-8&oe=UTF-8

[xviii] *The Sleeper Awakens,* p. 31.

[xix] *Cloud Skimmers.*

[xx] *Whisked Away,* June Whatley, Jurnee Books, 2021.

[xxi] *The Sleeper Awakens.*

[xxii] https://www.quantico.usmc-mccs.org/index.cfm/dining/the-clubs-at-quantico/

[xxiii] *Whisked Away.*

[xxiv] Psalm 91:4.

[xxv] Psalm 91:3 & 5.

[xxvi] Psalm 91:5

[xxvii] Psalm 91:16.

[xxviii] https://www.fbi.gov/services/training-academy, Hogan's Alley is a training complex simulating a small town where FBI and Drug Enforcement Administration (DEA) new agent trainees learn investigative techniques, firearms skills, and defensive tactics.

[xxix] Psalm 91:3.

[xxx] Jager is German for hunter.

[xxxi] Hebrews 13:2.

[xxxii] Luke 1:19.

[xxxiii] *Whisked Away.*

[xxxiv] Genesis 6:4.

[xxxv] 2 Peter 2:4.

[xxxvi] Genesis 6:4.

[xxxvii] Roman 6:23.

[xxxviii] *The Sleeper Awakens,* pp. 202-205.

[xxxix] *The Wizard of Oz* is a 1939 American musicalfantasy film produced by Metro-Goldwyn-Mayer. An adaptation of L. Frank Baum's 1900 children's fantasy novel *The Wonderful Wizard of Oz*, the film was primarily directed by Victor Fleming.

[xl] *Shackles*, by Mary, Mary. Songwriters: Erica Atkins-Campbell/Trecina Atkins-Campbell/Warryn Campbell. Shackles (Praise You) lyrics © Sony/ATV Music Publishing LLC, Universal Music Publishing Group, Warner Chappell Music, Inc.

[xli] 2 Samuel 6:14-16.

[xlii] Acts 16:25-26.

[xliii] *Shackles*, by Mary, Mary.

[xliv] *Shackles*, by Mary, Mary.

[xlv] Psalm 139:2.

[xlvi] 2 Samuel 6:14.

[xlvii] *Whisked Away.*

[xlviii] *From the D.E.E.P.,* p. 3.

[xlix] *The Sleeper Awakens.*

[l] *The Sleeper Awakens.*

[li] *Whisked Away,* pp. 98-99.

[lii] *Whisked Away.*

[liii] 17260 Rankin Ave, Dunlap, TN 37327

[liv] *From the D.E.E.P.*

[lv] Ephesians 6:12.

[lvi] Prayers and Declarations that Open the Courts of Heaven, Robert Henderson, Destiny Image books, October 16, 2018.

[lvii] https://www.news.com.au/lifestyle/real-life/true-stories/crime-capital-of-the-us-you-wont-find-on-a-map/news-story/93aa7388a17d3271a424a0202b21e73f

www.ingramcontent.com/pod-product-compliance
Lightning Source LLC
LaVergne TN
LVHW011949060526
838201LV00061B/4267